His smile was cold as he questioned Casey

"How long do you intend to stay in your newly discovered rural paradise, Miss Connolly?"

The question took her by surprise. "I have no idea."

"How long did you stay in your last job?"

She flinched, belatedly seeing the trap he was setting for her. "Six months," she said grudgingly, knowing her answer would simply confirm his belief that she was a rootless fly-by-nighter. She could hardly tell him she'd fled from a broken romance and a life-style that was becoming suffocating.

"Six months." He nodded slowly. "And how long have you been here?"

She tilted her head defiantly. "Eight months."

"So long? Congratulations, Miss Connolly—perhaps you've discovered the lure of permanency after all." He paused. "Until the next more glittering opportunity comes along."

Scottish-born **RACHEL ELLIOT** told her primary school teacher at the age of six that she wanted to be "a reporter—because I won't have to do any sums and I'll be able to write all the time." After the training grounds of university, journalism college, a provincial newspaper and a commercial radio station, she is now a reporter/presenter with Carlisle-based Border Television, which serves Cumbria, the Borders, Berwickshire, Southwest Scotland and the Isle of Man. Her mother and aunt live with her in Cumbria—along with three dogs, two budgies and the fulfillment of a childhood dream—a silver-gray Arab mare, Rhanna.

Books by Rachel Elliot

HARLEQUIN PRESENTS
1207—JOURNEY BACK TO LOVE

HARLEQUIN ROMANCE
2978—SONG OF LOVE

RACHEL ELLIOT

fantasy of love

Harlequin Books

TORONTO • NEW YORK • LONDON
AMSTERDAM • PARIS • SYDNEY • HAMBURG
STOCKHOLM • ATHENS • TOKYO • MILAN

Harlequin Presents first edition December 1991
ISBN 0-373-11415-X

Original hardcover edition published in 1990
by Mills & Boon Limited

FANTASY OF LOVE

CHAPTER ONE

As THE trailer rumbled away down the rutted farm road, Casey gave one last wave, then turned back towards the yard, impatience breaking her sneakered feet into a jog as she crossed to the stone outbuildings. At the stable door she stood for a moment, almost afraid to go in, lest it should all turn out to have been no more than a crazy dream.

Standing quietly in the stable, a pretty silvery grey mare gave a gentle whicker of welcome, and Casey smiled, her sherry-brown eyes lighting up with pleasure.

'So you really are here,' she murmured softly. 'It wasn't just a fantasy.'

Carefully she slid the bolt back and let herself in, making a valiant attempt to approach the animal calmly, even though her heart was thudding like that of a teenager in love. She raised one hand slowly to stroke the mare's velvety nose, her long fingers gentle.

'I've been waiting for you all of my life,' she said quietly. 'I started dreaming about you when I was just a kid—but it's taken me till the grand old age of twenty-seven to get you.' Her soft full lips curved into a wry smile. 'People will think I've gone totally mad, you know, especially Megan. What do you reckon?'

'I reckon they'll be completely convinced if I tell

them you've started talking to yourself on top of everything else!'

Startled, Casey swung round, her eyes widening in surprise at the unexpected voice. Then she started to chuckle, recognising the short, plump figure of her nearest neighbour.

'Lisa! I might have known it would be you. For a second I thought I'd bought myself a talking horse.'

'Aye, that'd have made a good story for your news programme, now.' Lisa's pale blue eyes crinkled at the corners in amusement. 'So it's true, then—you have got yourself an old nag.'

Casey grinned, knowing Lisa too well to take the barb seriously. The farmer's wife had been one of the first to welcome her into the closely knit rural community which had been her home for the past eight months since she'd come to work at the local television station, and, even though she was blessed with the straight-talking directness of all true Cumbrians, she also had one of the kindest hearts Casey had ever encountered.

'So you've already heard, huh?' Casey shook her head wonderingly, her short copper-coloured curls bobbing about her heart-shaped face. 'This place could easily make me redundant, you know—I swear you don't need television or journalists in this part of the world. News goes round by jungle drum.'

'Not always very accurately, though.' Lisa frowned as she leaned over the stable door. 'No one told me you'd bought an Arab.'

Casey gave an apologetic little smile. 'Maybe because I didn't much want to broadcast that particular detail.'

'I thought you fancied a nice docile little plodder.' Lisa slid her an assessing glance. A "bathchair on legs" was the phrase you used, I seem to remember.'

Casey laid a protective hand on the mare's neck. 'I know I did,' she said, her tone faintly defensive. 'But I hadn't bargained on coming across this little lady.'

'I assume you "came across her" at the horse sales?'

Casey nodded, a little shamefacedly, and Lisa sighed.

'Why on earth didn't you tell me you were going there to buy a horse? I'd have come with you.'

'I didn't go with the intention of buying anything. I went with a camera crew to do a report on the sales,' Casey explained. 'As part of the half-hour documentary I'm making on horses and riding in this region—I did tell you about it.'

Lisa nodded. 'So you did. But I never really imagined you'd end up buying an animal yourself.'

'Nor did I.' Casey met the other woman's eyes. 'But frankly, I'm relieved I managed to restrict myself to just one!'

Lisa chuckled. 'I know what you mean. Joe's all but forbidden me to go to any more sales, because I always end up heartbroken over the poor things that desperately need new homes. At least you managed to resist buying some broken-down old soul fit only for the knacker's yard.'

'Only because I walked round most of the time with my eyes shut,' Casey admitted ruefully. 'Otherwise I'd probably have bought the lot.'

'So how did you end up with this little lady?'

'I opened my eyes!' Casey smiled as Lisa's rich warm chuckle rang out. 'As soon as I saw her it was—well, I suppose it was love at first sight.'

'The worst of all possible reasons for buying a horse.' A slow, sweet smile lit Lisa's eyes. 'I've done it myself, though, so I do understand.' She paused, eyeing the mare. 'But an Arab?'

Casey flushed uncomfortably. 'You don't like the breed?'

Lisa shrugged. 'Like every other type of horse, you get good ones and bad ones. But they're hot-blooded and inclined to be rather temperamental, not really a beginner's horse—and you've said yourself, you're effectively a beginner.'

Casey nodded. 'I rode a lot as a kid, but I haven't ridden regularly for years. And I've never had a horse of my own.'

'Hmm. What's she like to ride?'

Casey looked down at the stable floor, scuffing a stray piece of straw with her foot. 'I don't know.'

'You haven't ridden her yet?' There was more than a touch of incredulity in Lisa's voice. 'You bought her without trying her out first?'

Casey nodded. 'I couldn't try her at the sales, because I wasn't properly dressed. But the man who sold her to me said she was fine, no vices at all.'

'Well, he would, wouldn't he?' Lisa shook her head slowly. 'Lord, but you really are a city girl, aren't you?'

Casey gave a rueful little shrug. 'I'm trying hard not to be.'

Lisa sighed. 'Well, what did the vet say? Did she at least get a clean bill of health?'

'I was afraid you were going to ask that.'

'You haven't had her vetted either.' There was no overt criticism in Lisa's words, merely resignation, yet Casey felt herself grow imperceptibly smaller.

'No.'

'Well, you must. I'll ring our vet for you first thing tomorrow morning, and ask him to have a look at her.' Lisa fixed Casey with a stern glance. 'But I warn you now, he's a straight-talking man. If she's no good, he won't pull any punches. So don't say I didn't warn you.'

Casey ran across the car park, her high heels clicking on the tarmac as she shouted a hasty farewell to her colleagues, ambling out of the building in a more leisurely manner, no doubt heading for the pub for their regular after-work drink. Of all the nights for Peter Brook to choose to conduct a post-mortem on the news programme, why did it have to be tonight? She'd really hoped she'd get home early, since Lisa had called to say the vet had agreed to come round in the evening to look at the mare.

'He wasn't too pleased, though,' she said. 'Wanted to know why you couldn't make a daytime appointment like everyone else.'

So on top of everything else she'd have some old grouch to contend with, who was annoyed at being kept from his pipe and slippers.

'Let's just hope he's professional enough not to let it colour his judgement,' Casey muttered aloud, catching sight of her own reflection in the rear-view mirror and groaning in irritation. Normally her first priority on leaving the studio after the teatime news magazine programme which she co-presented was to clean off all the make-up she'd never grown accustomed to wearing. Tonight she'd been in too much of a rush to bother, deciding she'd simply wipe most of it off on reaching home, before the vet arrived. Peter Brook had put paid to that with his interminable discussion on where the programme needed to be improved.

'I couldn't help thinking you seemed a bit distracted on screen tonight,' he'd told Casey. 'Did you have something on your mind?'

'Not a thing,' she'd lied blithely, knowing full well she'd gone through the entire show on automatic pilot, her thoughts centred entirely on a silver-grey Arab mare, and an anonymous vet who could pronounce her doom.

Not that she would let that happen, she swore fiercely, heading the car off the dual carriageway towards the village. Even if this straight-talking man found some minor defect in the pony, Casey was hell-bent on keeping her. But what if he finds a major problem? Irritated by the tiny voice niggling at the back of her mind, Casey stiffened her spine, a surge of protectiveness already preparing her to do battle with the man she hadn't even met yet.

An unfamiliar red car was parked in the yard when she finally got home, and the sight made her swear under her breath. Damn the man, couldn't he have been a little late too? If he'd been standing about drumming his heels, he'd doubtless be in an even more foul frame of mind.

The sound of laughter on the still summer air

stopped her in her tracks, then she heaved a great sigh of relief. She should have known Lisa wouldn't leave her to face this alone. She turned the corner heading for the stable, an apology already forming on her lips.

'Lisa, I'm so sorry I'm late. I just couldn't get away any earlier.'

Lisa, who was holding the mare by a long rope attached to her headcollar, gave Casey an unconcerned grin. 'No matter. I thought I'd come along in case my services were needed. 'Tisn't the first time I've acted as unpaid assistant, eh, Jamie?'

The vet, who had been hidden from view, bending over at the other side of the pony to inspect her legs, slowly straightened up as Casey switched on the regulation 'polite smile' she normally reserved for potentially troublesome interviewees. The smile froze on her lips as her eyes travelled upwards over a powerful chest straining the white cotton shirt that covered it, to incredibly wide shoulders, and upwards again to a face that could have been carved from granite. It wasn't a handsome face, she decided hazily, but it was a strong one, its every feature decided and distinct. His eyes were dark blue and direct, clearly accustomed to looking every man straight in the face. His mouth, hewn by the hand of a master, might have been capable of tenderness, but there was little sign of that in its current tight-lipped mode. As he looked at Casey, there was nothing in his expression but a coolly contemptuous dislike.

'Well, well,' he drawled unpleasantly. 'I didn't realise my new client was a television star.'

'Hardly that.' Casey tried to make a laughing disclaimer, but he shook his head.

'Don't pretend false modesty, Miss Connolly. It doesn't befit a celebrity.'

Lisa shot him a questioning look, clearly puzzled by his attitude. 'Didn't I mention Casey's job?' she queried. 'Sorry—we're all so accustomed to her about here, we tend to forget her TV life.'

'And that's just the way I like——'

'How very unkind of you Lisa.' It was as if Casey hadn't even spoken. 'I'm sure our star can't enjoy having her status dismissed so lightly.'

'On the contrary,' Casey retorted, stung by his words. 'You're the only one who seems at all concerned with my so-called status.'

'Really?' His dark eyes flickered over her and she bore the scrutiny uncomfortably, suddenly feeling completely out of place in the stable-yard, wearing her elegant red suit and high-heeled sandals. 'Then I assume you expect your appearance to establish your status for you?'

'Look, I don't normally dress like this——'

'For heaven's sake, would you two stop bickering?' Lisa's normally placid features had taken on an uncharacteristically irritated scowl. 'This poor pony's standing here like an angel, but I can't guarantee she will for much longer.'

The man's rigid features relaxed into a grin as he turned away from Casey. 'Right as usual,' he said cheerfully. 'The animal is the important one here, even if she doesn't appear on the small screen.'

Casey clenched her hands into fists, gripped by a feeling of sheer frustration. For two pins she'd have told the arrogant devil to pack his veterinary kit and get out, but concern for the pony kept her quiet. Even if she had taken an immediate dislike to him, he had been recommended by Lisa, and even to her inexperienced eye it was clear he knew what he was doing.

'So you bought her without benefit of a vet's examination, Miss Connolly?'

She gritted her teeth and nodded mutely.

'You thought you knew better than a vet?'

'It wasn't like that,' she muttered ungraciously. 'I simply liked her, that's all. It was all done purely on impulse.'

He nodded sagely. 'Just as you would buy a new dress, perhaps, or a hat?' His gaze flickered over her and she shrank before the undisguised distaste in his deep blue eyes.

Lisa sent her a sympathetic look. 'Come off it, Jamie,' she said. 'You know I've done the same thing myself, and you've never given me such a hard time for it.'

'But you knew what you were doing.' Casey felt herself pinned by his piercing look. 'Miss Connolly did not.'

'Look, Mr. . .' she hesitated, belatedly realising she hadn't been told his surname, 'I asked you to come here to give me your professional opinion on this animal, and to tell me whether or not she's sound. I don't recall asking for any comments on me.' She took a deep breath. 'You appear to have something against television journalists, but frankly I don't much care what you think of me, my profession, or my actions. It's the mare that counts.'

'I couldn't agree more.' He straightened up to his full height, towering over Casey, even in her high heels. 'But you must understand—in my years as a vet, I've come across a great many mistreated animals.'

'I would never mistreat her!' Casey was cut to the heart by the very suggestion.

He held up one hand imperiously. 'Not deliberately, perhaps. But cruelty comes in many guises— one of them being sheer ignorance. Just how much do you actually know about looking after horses? Have you ever owned one before?'

'No,' she conceded reluctantly. 'But then I've lived in cities since I was quite young. I've never had the chance.'

'But now you find yourself in the country, so you've decided a horse is the perfect accessory to go with your Barbour jacket and Hunter wellingtons.' His upper lip curled slightly. 'Let me put something to you, Miss Connolly. Most people, and perhaps especially those born to the country life, seek stability, firm foundations, something solid to build on. In my experience, journalists tend to be just the opposite. They positively thrive on a lack of security and routine——'

'Is there a point to all of this?' Casey broke in impatiently. 'If so, would you mind very much getting to it?'

He smiled coldly. 'How long do you intend to stay in your new-found rural paradise, Miss Connolly?'

The question took her by surprise. 'I have no idea.'

'How long did you stay in your last job?'

She flinched, belatedly seeing the trap he was setting for her. 'Six months,' she said grudgingly, hating the way that sounded. She knew perfectly well her answer would simply confirm his belief that she was a rootless fly-by-night, but not for anything would she tell this boorish oaf the real reason for her short stay in London. Somehow she couldn't see him sympathising if she said she'd fled from a broken romance and a lifestyle that was fast becoming suffocating. A man of granite, such as he obviously imagined himself to be, would doubtless have stayed there through sheer cussedness.

'Six months.' He nodded slowly. 'And how long have you been here?'

She tilted her head defiantly. 'Eight months.'

His eyebrows lifted mockingly, disappearing beneath an unruly fringe of wavy dark hair that seemed somehow out of keeping with the stern rigidity of his features. 'So long? Congratulations, Miss Connolly—perhaps you've discovered the lure of permanency after all.' He paused, his eyes flickering over her. 'Until the next, more glittering opportunity comes along, that is.'

'Look,' Casey squared up to him, unconsciously stiffening her spine as she prepared to defend herself, 'you've clearly reached your own conclusions about me, and I'm not about to tackle the obviously fruitless task of trying to change your mind—however, doesn't it tell you anything about me that I came to work here after leaving a job in London— the so-called city of opportunity?'

He gave her a considering look. 'That tells me

you preferred to be a big fish in a little pool rather than vice versa, Miss Connolly,' he said slowly. 'A pretty astute career move, many would say.' Before Casey could muster a reply, he stepped back from the mare. 'Enough of this. Take the lead-rein—I want to see her trot.'

'I'll do that, Jamie,' Lisa began, but he quelled her with a look.

'The pony is Miss Connolly's new toy,' he said in a soft voice that made Casey's flesh creep. 'Let's see if she knows how it works.'

Casey felt a sudden sting of angry tears in her eyes. Why was he so hell-bent on humiliating her? In her pencil-line red skirt and insubstantial high-heeled sandals, she certainly wasn't dressed properly for running alongside ponies, and he knew it. She glared back at him mutinously, about to refuse, but the challenging gleam in his dark eyes changed her mind.

'Certainly,' she said stiffly. 'Come on, girl!' Affecting a confidence she was far from feeling, she took the lead-rein and sent up a silent thanks as the mare obligingly began to walk at her side.

'I asked you to make her trot, Miss Connolly.' The vet's voice followed her down the yard. 'I need to see how freely she moves.'

Muttering a heartfelt oath under her breath, Casey broke into a jog, tugging gently on the lead rein.

'Faster, please.'

She speeded up as much as her restrictive skirt would allow. They reached the end of the yard and were halfway back down when a stray breeze sent a piece of paper fluttering under the mare's nose and she shied to the side, knocking into Casey, who stumbled over her right ankle.

'Are you OK?' Lisa was at her side in an instant, her pale blue eyes concerned.

'Just fine.' Casey bit her lip, refusing to acknowledge the pain in her ankle. 'My own fault—I should have seen that coming.'

'Here, let me take the rein.'

'No.' Casey shook her head stubbornly. 'I'll lead her back.'

Lisa grinned. 'Don't let Jamie get to you,' she advised. 'He may sound like a bad-tempered bear, but his heart's in the right place really.'

'Heart?' Casey muttered, trying not to wince visibly as she put her weight on her right foot. 'I doubt very much if the unfeeling swine possesses such a thing!'

Lisa shook her head, her eyes serious. 'You're wrong. But perhaps you'll eventually find that out for yourself.' She smiled brightly as they rejoined Jamie. 'What do you think, vet-man? Will she pass muster?'

'She'll do,' he returned tersely, his eyes on Casey. 'What about you? How's your ankle?'

'It's fine.' Surprise at his apparent concern robbed her of the irritation she'd been building up against him. 'I just turned it slightly, that's all.'

'Let me see.'

Casey's heart skipped a definite beat as he knelt down before her. 'Honestly, it's perfectly OK. I——'

'Let me be the judge of that.' He glanced up at

her. 'And don't worry—I may be an animal doctor, but I do have a basic knowledge of the human anatomy.'

'I didn't——'

'Lean on Lisa for a moment.' He lifted her foot on to his bent knee, his long, capable fingers gently probing her ankle. Casey's eyes widened as his touch sent an unexpected heat flooding through her veins. 'I don't think you've done any damage,' he said after a moment, carefully setting her foot back on the ground. 'It may be slightly swollen tomorrow, so you'd better wear more sensible footwear for a couple of days.' For the first time since they'd met he smiled at her, a warm and genuine smile that stripped the harshness from his features and made the breath catch in her throat. He should smile more often, she thought irrelevantly. It makes him look almost handsome.

'There's nothing wrong with these shoes.' Annoyance at her own reactions made her voice sharp. 'But they weren't designed for running alongside ponies.'

He nodded, a humorous glint in his eyes. 'I know, and I apologise. I shouldn't have asked you to do it.'

Casey opened her mouth to give him a scathing reply, then closed it again abruptly, thrown off balance by his unexpected climb-down.

'Incidentally, do you have papers for her?'

Casey shook her head. 'The man said her previous owner had lost them.'

'Pity.' He gave the mare one last look-over. 'Probably against all the odds, it would seem you've bought a nice little animal. She's perfectly sound and healthy, a little on the thin side perhaps, but nothing that a few weeks on good grass won't put right.' The momentary warmth disappeared from his expression. 'So kindly don't let your false pride harm her, Miss Connolly. She deserves very much better than that.'

Casey met his gaze evenly. 'She'll be well looked after.'

He nodded. 'I hope so,' he said. 'For your sake as well as hers, I hope so.'

'Lord, I felt as if I were back in school again, under the eagle eyes of the headmaster!' Casey kicked off her sandals and padded across the kitchen floor on stocking-soled feet. 'Is he always like that?'

Lisa took two cups from the pantry and spooned coffee powder into both. 'Not usually quite as overbearing,' she said. 'He seemed to be laying it on thick for your benefit. Where have you hidden the sugar this time?'

'Sugar?' Casey's forehead creased in a puzzled frown. 'Haven't a clue. It hasn't been used since last time you were here.'

'I found it in the bread bin then.' Lisa shook her head with good-natured exasperation. 'I can never understand how you manage to be so organised and efficient at work——'

'And a total disaster at home,' Casey finished for her. 'It is pretty ridiculous, I know. I suppose it's because my sister Megan did all the housekeeping for such a long time in our home.' She sat down at the kitchen table, propping her chin on her hands, a distant expression in her sherry-brown eyes. 'I was only eleven when our parents died, she was seventeen. Right from the start she refused to let me do anything about the house—said that was her domain, and my job was to do well at school and pass all my exams.' She gave a wistful little smile. 'Our folks set great store by education, but Megan never really liked school much, so I suppose she thought it was up to her to give me every possible chance.'

'I left school as soon as I possibly could.' Lisa finally located the sugar bowl in the fridge and spooned a generous quantity into her cup. 'All I ever wanted to do was work with animals.' She laughed. 'Jamie and I always had that in common— but he had brains and I didn't, so he became a vet and I became a dogsbody.'

'You and he went to school together?' Casey was astounded to feel a sharp stab of something unaccountably like jealousy.

'Uh-huh. He was a couple of years ahead of me, same age as my big brother, but all of us country kids hung about together in one big group.'

'Did you have a crush on him?' Casey leaned back against the Aga range, strangely reluctant to hear the answer to her own question.

'Who didn't?' Lisa's eyes all but disappeared as a broad grin creased her plump cheeks. 'Tall, dark, good-looking as Lucifer—the girls were all crazy for him!'

Casey managed to produce a laugh. 'Now I understand how you can be so familiar with him. Personally I can't even imagine calling him by his christian name.'

'You could if you'd seen him dripping wet and stark naked after skinny-dipping in the river, or watched him rolling in the hay with one of his countless girlfriends.'

'You watched him?'

Lisa nodded, her eyes twinkling with remembered mischief. 'Through a peephole in the floor from the loft above the barn. It was a favourite pastime—till we discovered for ourselves just what was so much fun about rolling in the hay, that is! Jamie was a devil—had his pick of all the lasses in the neighbourhood. Not one could say no to him.'

'What about you?' Casey toyed unconcernedly with the spoon in the sugar bowl.

Lisa shook her head regretfully. 'He never asked me. He treated me as a little sister—much to my eternal disgust! Maybe it was just as well, though— he broke a lot of hearts in his time. Even when the rest of us were beginning to pair off, he seemed reluctant to commit himself for any length of time to just one girl. But every new conquest hoped she'd be the one to snare him.'

'It's hard for me to imagine him doing anything as human and irresponsible as having a lark in the hay with a girl.' Casey gave a little self-conscious chuckle. 'I can't even come to terms with his being called Jamie.'

'Why ever not?'

Casey shrugged. 'The name conjures up someone gentle and kind—not a dark, forbidding character like him.'

'He can be very gentle and kind.' Lisa was quick to defend her childhood friend. 'You only have to

see him with animals to realise that.' She pinned
Casey with a faintly accusing look. 'Come to that,
you've already had personal experience of it.'

'I have?'

Lisa nodded. 'When he examined your ankle. He
wasn't exactly rough, was he?'

'Well, no, I——'

'I rest my case.' Lisa sat back, folding her arms in
obvious satisfaction. 'Anyway, why all the great
interest in Jamie? I could have sworn you'd taken
an instant dislike to him.'

Casey looked down at the table, uncomfortable
under the other woman's narrow-eyed scrutiny. 'I
did,' she said. 'And you're wrong, I'm not particularly interested in him. I was just curious to know
why he seemed so unfriendly towards me, that's all.'

For a long moment Lisa stared into her empty
coffee-cup. 'Perhaps because you remind him of
someone he used to know,' she said at last. It was
clear from the rigid set of her shoulders that she was
uneasy giving even that much information away.

'Who was she?' Casey queried softly. 'A
girlfriend?'

Lisa shook her head. 'I'm sorry,' she said decidedly, 'the story isn't mine to tell. I'd rather you
heard it from Jamie.'

Casey bit back her growing curiosity. 'Then I'll
probably never hear it,' she said brightly. 'Because,
quite frankly, I have no intention of ever seeing, let
alone speaking to the man again if I can help it.
One head-on collision with a brick wall is quite
enough, thank you!'

Lisa slid her a measuring look. 'Don't be too sure

about that, missy,' she said. 'I reckon your paths will cross again.' Seeing Casey's startled look, she smiled. 'Don't forget, it's a small world. And this little corner of it is perhaps even smaller than most.'

'I've been here for eight months without seeing him,' Casey returned stubbornly. 'I reckon it's big enough to contain us both without any more collisions.'

That night she was unusually restless, couldn't sleep. Tossing and turning, she pounded the pillow irritably, but every time she closed her eyes it was to see all over again the vet's darkly brooding expression—or, worse, the apparent contempt in his dark eyes when he looked at her. Why on earth had he taken such an instantaneous dislike to her? OK, so she'd arrived late, and she hadn't been dressed properly for the occasion, but she'd apologised for that. It hardly seemed sufficient grounds for him to despise her.

In the darkness of her bedroom she frowned. Why should she care? A man she'd never met before and probably wouldn't meet again had disliked her. So what? Heaven knew, in her job as a journalist, she should be accustomed to people making snap judgements on her. Certainly there were those who had been on the receiving end of her reporter's interrogative techniques who wouldn't exactly queue to join her fan club. That was an unfortunate but unavoidable fact of her life. She'd never lost sleep over it before. But at least in those situations she'd been able to understand the reasons behind the dislike. For the life of her she couldn't begin to fathom the reasons behind the vet's coldness. And, without doubt, it bothered her.

Perhaps that had something to do with Lisa—and with the wider issue of her acceptance by the local people. That they'd welcomed her into their close-knit community meant a great deal to her, and she cherished the warmth of the friendship Lisa had offered from the start. Would she change her mind after seeing Jamie's reaction? He was, after all, an old and obviously valued friend, while Casey was a relative newcomer.

She shook her head, tired of the crowding images fogging her brain. She was being ridiculous. Lisa was an adult woman, perfectly capable of making up her own mind. She wouldn't allow herself to be swayed. Casey resolutely closed her eyes. Let Jamie whatever-his-name-was go to hell. He couldn't hurt her. She hoped.

CHAPTER TWO

NEXT morning Casey was halfway across the yard, only part awake and dressed in an old pair of jeans and a comfortably baggy sweatshirt, when the sight of a tall, dark-haired man standing by the field gate brought her abruptly to consciousness. There was no mistaking that powerful, commanding figure—it had been plaguing her dreams all night. But what on earth was he doing here at this time of day—had something happened to the mare? Her heart was beating a rapid tattoo as she broke into a run.

'Good morning.' His eyes swept over her flushed cheeks and tousled hair. 'Just up? You're missing the best part of the day.'

'What's wrong with the pony?' Too alarmed to bother with polite greetings, she blurted out the question.

'Wrong?' He looked puzzled. 'Nothing, as far as I can see. Why?'

Confused, Casey shook her head. 'I thought. . .'

'That since I was here, something must have happened to her?' The unexpected warmth of his smile made something move deep inside her. 'Hardly, Miss Connolly. We vets are many things, but we don't generally claim to be psychic as well. No, I simply thought you might be taking advantage of this fine morning by having an early ride. Obviously I was wrong.'

'I don't have any tack for her yet,' Casey returned, a little defensively.

His lips tightened. 'I suppose that was predictable,' he said at last. 'Are you intending to get any, or is she to be kept as a pretty ornament in the field?'

'Of course not!' She bridled at the sarcasm in his voice. So the momentary spark of compassion she'd seen a moment ago had fled already—or had she simply imagined it? 'Lisa's going to loan me tack till I can buy my own.'

'Lisa.' He nodded knowingly. 'Once again she comes to your rescue.' The dark blue eyes regarded her steadily. 'Are you going to ask Lisa to ride her for you as well?'

'No, I'm not!' Irritation finally snapped her patience. 'And frankly, Mr. . .'

'Oliver,' he supplied obligingly. 'But you can call me Jamie.'

'Mr Oliver,' she continued through gritted teeth, 'I really don't see that any of this is any of your business. It's surely up to me to decide what I do with the pony. She does belong to me, after all.'

'And I won't hesitate to get her taken away from you if you prove incapable of looking after her.' His eyes were like dark granite, cold and hard, and she felt a touch of despair. Just what did she have to do to get through to this man? She took a deep breath before replying.

'You have no grounds whatsoever to suspect I won't look after her,' she said evenly. 'But, for reasons best known to yourself, you seem hell-bent on finding me guilty and hanging me before I've even committed a crime. I don't know why, and I'm not sure I really care, but I would be grateful if you'd simply leave now, and stop putting a blight on what was a perfectly fine morning.'

She turned to walk away, but he grabbed her arm, making her wince as his fingers dug into her tender flesh.

'I'll leave with pleasure,' he said with quiet malevolence. 'It doesn't brighten my day to spend the first part of it with a spoiled, self-indulgent brat who can't even get out of bed in the morning.' His voice, low and even, carried an unmistakable threat. 'Just be sure of this—I'll be keeping an eye on you, Miss Connolly. As far as I'm concerned, the quicker you become tired of the country life you're currently amusing yourself with, and return to the city where you really belong, the better for all concerned— especially that pony.' For a long moment he stared deep into her eyes as though searching for something. She desperately wanted to move away, but somehow she was held, mesmerised by his gaze, anchored to him by his relentless grip on her arm.

'Why do you dislike me so much?' The words almost seemed to say themselves.

'Dislike you?' The question apparently surprised him. 'I don't particularly dislike *you*, Miss Connolly —I simply detest your kind.'

'I'm an individual, Mr Oliver,' she stated quietly, the continued warmth of his fingers on her arm making her heart beat in a crazily erratic rhythm. 'I don't know what you mean by "my kind", but I don't appreciate being lumped in with any group of people.'

'Yet it's doubtless what you do to all the poor saps you interview.'

Casey frowned. 'I don't know what you mean. When I meet someone for the first time, I assess him or her as a person. I don't make snap judgements, or pin labels on people.'

'Don't you?' His eyes were coolly mocking now. 'I'd suggest you make up your mind before you even leave the office, so that you can determine your tactics. Presumably you'd take a different line of approach to a farmer than to an executive, for instance?'

'Well, yes, but that's only common sense,' Casey returned hotly. 'There's nothing devious about that.'

'Nothing devious, perhaps,' he agreed. 'But isn't it patronising in the extreme to assume you know a person's character simply because of the job they do?'

'If you put it that way, then yes,' Casey cut in. 'And that's exactly——'

'What I've been doing to you.' He leaned languidly back against the fence, clearly enjoying the verbal sparring match. 'Do you also find that in the vast majority of cases your initial assumptions prove correct?'

Casey's eyes narrowed. She could see where this was leading to, but couldn't for the life of her see any means of backing out now. 'Yes, I do,' she conceded reluctantly, 'but——'

'Then you really can't take me to task for using the same criteria in assessing you,' he finished, with a smug arrogance that infuriated her.

'But there's one major difference between you and me,' she forced herself to speak calmly. 'I'm capable of changing my mind if I discover I've been wrong.'

'And you think I couldn't?' The jet-black eyebrows quirked humorously.

'No, I don't believe you could,' she returned evenly. 'I think your sense of self-conceit would never allow you to admit you'd been mistaken about anything.' She paused, slowly shaking her head. 'And that's really rather sad, Mr Oliver. Just think of all the opportunities for friendship you could lose through your blindness.'

'Opportunities?' He seemed to savour the word. 'You mean—like this?'

Before she had time to realise what he had in mind, he clasped her by the shoulders and pulled her roughly against his solid frame. She gave a startled squawk of protest, but even as she looked up at him in outraged astonishment, he bent over her, one hand cupping the back of her head to draw her closer still. His lips, incredibly tender, found her own, and for one dizzying moment the whole world seemed to skid to a halt. The only thing she was conscious of was the feeling of his mouth moving against hers, probing, softly searching, his tongue seeking entrance, and finding no barrier, playfully teasing. She tried desperately to find the strength to push him away, but the feeling of his lips robbed her of resistance, demolished her defences. When he finally lifted his head there was an unmistakable gleam of triumph in the dark depths of his eyes. Dazed by the tender assault he had launched so unexpectedly, she could only stare up at him, knowing her cheeks were flushed, her lips still bearing the brand of his possession.

'Why did you do that?' she whispered.

He grinned. 'Because I hate to miss out on opportunities,' he said, with an undented self-assurance that wounded her more deeply than any of his earlier barbs. For a second the temptation to slap the smug look from his face was almost too much to resist. It was galling in the extreme to realise she'd been shaken to the core by his kisses, while he obviously hadn't been affected at all.

'Then I hope you made the most of it,' she said, bitterness dripping like acid into her voice. 'Because it's an opportunity that will never come your way again!'

She turned on her heel then and strode away towards the field gate, her head held high as his mocking laughter rang out behind her.

'So what's turned you into such a grouch today? I haven't seen you smile once all morning.'

Casey looked up from the typewriter with a frown. 'I'm trying to write scripts for the half-hour special on horses,' she said shortly. 'I've been concentrating, that's all.'

'Bull!' Disbelieving grey eyes smiled down into her own. 'I've been watching you—you haven't typed a single word since you put the paper into the machine.'

Casey sighed heavily. 'I'm finding inspiration hard to come by, that's all. I haven't been slacking, if that's what you think.'

'Hey, hey, what's this?' Peter Brook perched himself on the edge of her desk and laid a friendly hand on her shoulder. 'I wasn't attempting to lay the Heavy Boss routine on you—just showing a bit of neighbourly concern, is all.'

Casey managed with an effort to bite back a grin at the news editor's choice of words. A sabbatical year spent in the United States had left him with an indelible legacy of American slang expressions which sounded comical in his rich Cumbrian accent.

'I know,' she replied gently. 'And it's good of you to be concerned, but there's no need, I promise.' Seeing his eyebrows raise in mild reproof, she gave a tiny shrug of her narrow shoulders. 'Oh, all right— I had a bit of a run-in with one of the local worthies, and it's been preying on my mind ever since, but that's all there is to it.'

'Aha!' Peter nodded knowingly. 'Trouble in your rural paradise at last. Well, haven't I told you all along it was a mistake to hide yourself away in the sticks? You should be living in the city, where everything happens.'

Casey frowned, remembering James Oliver had also scathingly referred to her "rural paradise". Why was it so hard for both men to believe she was living where she wanted to live, not because it was fashionable, or even a form of escape, but simply because she loved the place?

'So what have you done, then? Run over a hen? Given refuge to a fox? Accidentally let a prize bullock run amok? What is it—for goodness' sake put me out of my misery!'

'None of the above!' Casey held up one hand to

stop the flow of words. 'I had something of a disagreement with the local vet, that's all.'

'All? All?' Peter slid off the desk, gazing down at her in apparent dismay. 'Don't you know the worst thing you can possibly do in a rural community is fall out with the vet? They hold great local influence, you know.' He shook his head slowly. 'In fact, probably the only crime more heinous is to argue with the secretary of the local WI.'

Casey smiled, refusing to take him seriously. 'You'll be telling me it's a hanging crime next!'

'It probably still is in some counties,' he returned solemnly. 'Believe me, I know what I'm talking about. I once tried to stand up for myself against a vet—he and my wife ganged up on me over our Yorkshire Terrorist.'

Casey shot him a puzzled look. 'Don't you mean Yorkshire Terrier?'

'I know exactly what I mean—the dog's an absolute little villain! Anyway, I didn't have a leg to stand on—the two of them together could have put all of Ghengis Khan's hordes to flight!'

By now Casey was laughing out loud, scripts forgotten as Peter's words conjured up crazy pictures in her mind. 'Do you realise you're completely bonkers?' she queried.

He nodded, quite unabashed. 'Course I do. It's an essential requirement if you want to be a news editor.' He favoured her with an enormous wink. 'But don't laugh at all my words, young miss—some of them were meant to be taken seriously, and what I said at first was perfectly true. If you've moved into a small community, it's never a good idea to upset its stalwarts. They're the ones who can make life hell for you.'

His advice was still ringing in her mind as she drove home that evening, largely because she knew perfectly well it held more than a grain of truth. Being accepted into the tiny Cumbrian village had been important right from the first day when Lisa had appeared at her door, grinning widely and offering to help unpack boxes. She'd been the first to offer the hand of friendship, but others hadn't been slow to follow, and Casey had always been grateful, particularly after her time in London, where she'd felt like a total outsider. Their acceptance wasn't something she simply took for granted, however, since she was, and always would be, a newcomer—or an 'offcomer', as the Cumbrians said.

Now there was Jamie Oliver, threatening not only to be a thorn in her flesh, but who could easily damage her standing locally. It was a depressing thought. Admittedly, it didn't seem likely she'd bump into him again in the foreseeable future, but perhaps when they did meet next it would be a wise idea to count to ten and do her utmost to treat him with cool, unreproachable politeness. If only the man weren't so damned infuriating! In just two short meetings he'd already managed to get under her skin and send her temper flaring. She'd just have to hope their paths didn't cross again till she'd managed to get her reactions under some kind of control.

Satisfied with her decision, she drove into the courtyard, and was horrified to discover she'd been

half hoping to see the vet's familiar red car parked
there. Finding the place empty brought both a rush
of relief and a pang of disappointment, though it
was hard to admit as much, even to herself.

Eager to get out to the pony, she postponed
thoughts of dinner, and changed quickly into jeans
and a sweatshirt, hastily pulling a brush through her
tangled copper curls. The early evening air, still and
balmy, had an instantly soothing effect on nerves
which seemed to have been on edge since the
morning's encounter with James Oliver, and she
breathed deeply, stopping for a moment to look out
over the lush green fields and valleys surrounding
her home, enjoying the tranquillity of the moment.

The feeling lasted until she walked into the stone
building which housed the stable, only to stop in her
tracks at the sight of a saddle placed neatly against
one wall, and a bridle hanging from the peg above.
Attached to the peg was a note from Lisa.

'Here's the gear as promised,' it read. 'I've
already tried it on the pony and it fits perfectly.
Incidentally, when are you going to come up with a
name for the poor animal—we can't keep calling
her the pony! Let me know how you get on—you'll
find the best way is via the stirrups.'

Casey stared at the tack, her stomach suddenly
crowded with fluttering butterflies. This was it—the
great moment had arrived—the moment when she
had to find out exactly what sort of animal she'd
bought. It was what she'd been longing for ever
since she first spotted the silvery grey mare at the
sales, yet now it was here she was dismayed to find
she was afraid. That was ridiculous—she'd bought

the mare to ride and, after all, she wasn't a complete novice. As a youngster she'd been on horseback whenever she could get the chance. But that was then, a tiny voice whispered in her brain. Now is different.

For a long moment she simply stood in the silent stable, gazing at the bridle as though it could provide the answers. Perhaps the wisest thing would be to wait till Lisa could be there—to provide moral support if nothing else. Wouldn't James Oliver just love that? the tiny voice mocked. He already thinks you're completely hopeless; that would simply confirm it.

The thought of the vet and his sarcastic comments was enough to spur her into action. Damn the man—he'd been plaguing her all day, his dark features constantly niggling at the back of her mind. The conversation with Peter Brook hadn't helped either—it had simply left her more confused than ever.

'But actually, there's nothing to be confused about,' she muttered aloud as she clambered over the gate into the field. 'The man's a total skunk, even if he does have Lisa and every other woman for miles around eating out of his hand. Well, he won't add me to his list of devoted admirers, that's for sure!'

The pony stood quietly as Casey slipped a head-collar over her ears and attached a long lead-rope.

'So far so good, little lady.' She fondled the animal's ears affectionately. 'You carry on like this, and we'll be just fine.'

Talking quietly to her all the time, she led the

mare out of the field and over to the stable, tying her up loosely before giving her a quick rub over with one of the brushes Lisa had loaned her.

'So tell me, what did you think of Jamie Oliver?' Casey knew perfectly well she was talking in a bid to cover up her own nerves. 'Don't suppose you really had much reason to complain did you? He liked you.' She chuckled at her own words—an eavesdropper would probably think she was jealous—of a pony! 'Who knows, sweetheart?' She eased the bit into the mare's mouth and buckled up the bridle. 'Maybe I am at that—just a little bit.'

Minutes later, after checking over the tack for the umpteenth time, Casey grabbed her whip and took several long steadying breaths.

'We're only going to go in the field,' she smiled as the animal's ears flicked back at the sound of her voice, 'so, if you decide to buck me off, at least I'll have a reasonably soft landing.' Leading the mare by the reins, she walked to the field, then carefully hoisted herself into the saddle, her tension easing slightly as the pony stood still as a statue for her to mount. 'We're going to be just fine, sweetheart,' she murmured, feeling an unmistakable surge of elation mixed in with the fear. 'Walk on, now.'

Given the command, the mare began to dance a little, and Casey instinctively grabbed on the reins, her legs gripping the animal's sides.

'You're doing all the right things to get yourself bucked off.' A calm, lazy voice floated through the evening air and Casey turned her head slightly, feeling a strange sense of inevitability as she saw Jamie Oliver standing by the gate.

'She's a little bit fresh.'

'Well, of course she is.' His lips quirked into a faint smile. 'Probably hasn't been ridden in weeks.' He leaned his weight against the gate. 'Would you like me to ride her for a little while? Get some of the fizz out of her?'

'No, thank you.' Pride stiffened Casey's spine, even though she was sorely tempted to accept the offer.

He shrugged. 'Suit yourself. If I were you, then, I'd give her her head for a little while. You'll never get any sense out of her while she's like that.'

As if in agreement, the pony skittered forward a few steps, then, apparently frustrated by Casey's restraining hands on the reins, ducked her head forward and gave a tiny buck. Casey managed to sit it out, but her heart was in her mouth by the time she'd managed to bring the animal under control again.

'She's only playing. She didn't mean anything nasty by that buck—it was a very half-hearted effort.'

Even though his presence was infuriating, Casey found herself reassured by his calm air of authority.

'Ride her on,' he called now. 'She'll only buck again if you keep her standing still.'

Offering up a silent prayer, Casey squeezed gently with her legs, half expecting to end up in the next county. The mare obligingly stepped forward, and she heaved a deep sigh of grateful relief. This pace she could handle. Within minutes, though, the pony had broken into a jog—obviously the sedate stuff wasn't going to suit her at all.

'OK, honey,' Casey muttered under her breath.
'Let's stretch it out a little—only let's not break any
speed records, please!'

The pony needed no second bidding. Given her
head, she broke quickly from trot to canter, her
hoofs eating up the ground as she sped on. On her
back, Casey clung on for dear life, grabbing a
handful of mane for extra support. Her feet had
come out of the stirrups in the first few strides, and
now her legs were clamped to the mare's sides in a
vice-like grip, even though she knew perfectly well
that would be interpreted as a signal to go faster
still.

On her second circuit of the field she caught a
glimpse of Jamie Oliver, his expression openly
amused as he watched, and the sight sent a spurt of
anger shooting through her. So the son-of-a-bitch
was enjoying himself, was he? Well, she'd be
damned if she'd play still further into his hands by
falling off!

After that, it was a mixture of fear, self-preser-
vation and sheer cussedness that kept her in the
saddle, until the pony finally began to tire, and put
the brakes on for herself. Not at all looking forward
to Jamie Oliver's inevitable sarcasm, Casey held her
head high as she trotted sedately back across the
field.

'Well done!'

She was completely taken aback by the
compliment.

'Well done?'

His dark eyes glinted humorously. 'I didn't say
well ridden—you just sat there like a sack of

potatoes. But at least you stayed in the saddle.' He eyed her thoughtfully. 'Were you afraid?'

She lifted her head defiantly, stubborn pride sending a denial to her lips. But his challenging expression defeated her.

'Terrified.'

There was genuine warmth in his smile as he nodded slowly. 'Can't say I blame you. It is frightening when you know you're not in control.'

Casey gathered up the reins in one hand, preparing to dismount.

'What do you think you're doing?'

She looked up, surprised by the question. 'What does it look as if I'm doing? I'm getting off.'

'If you get off now, you might as well start looking for another buyer right away, because you'll never find the courage to get back in the saddle again.' His expression was unreadable. 'It's up to you, Casey. Do you want to be able to ride this pony?'

'Of course I do, but surely——'

'Then this is where the work begins.' He climbed easily over the fence and went to the mare's head, stroking her nose tenderly. 'And I do mean work,' he warned. 'This is no riding school slouch accustomed to plodding round in circles all day long. She won't let you off with half-hearted riding. So come on, trot her back into the middle of the field, and I'll put you both through your paces.'

'Why are you doing this?' Casey said wonderingly. 'Why on earth should you care whether I can ride or not?'

'Don't be misled, Miss Connolly.' The momentary warmth had fled—apparently he'd forgotten

he'd used her christian name just a few moments
ago, and she found herself regretting his return to
the formal address. 'I don't much care if you can
ride or not, but I do care about the pony. I don't
want to see a perfectly nice animal end up in the
knacker's yard simply because you can't handle her
and you don't know what else to do with her.' He
slid her a measuring glance. 'Incidentally, are you
ever going to grace her with a name?'

More wounded by his words than she would ever
allow herself to admit, Casey nodded, a lingering
vestige of pride making her tilt her chin defiantly
upward. 'Yes, I am,' she said quietly, searching
desperately in her mind for inspiration. She'd been
trying for days to come up with a good name, with
no success, but she wasn't about to admit that to
him. 'She's called Fantasy,' she said at last.

He shook his head slowly. 'Somehow your choice
of name doesn't surprise me in the least. It just sums
up what she is to you, doesn't it? Not a living,
breathing creature at all—but a dream. Well,
beware, Miss Connolly, for fantasies are but fleeting
things.' He paused. 'Are you ready?'

She nodded mutely.

'Then trot on.'

Hours later Casey crawled into bed, almost too tired
to stretch out a hand to switch off the lamp. Only
the awareness that she'd be stiff as a board and
aching in every muscle the following day had driven
her to have a hot bath before turning in for the
night, for she couldn't remember ever feeling more
exhausted in her life.

'Lord, what a slave-driver the man is!' she groaned aloud, easing her tired limbs into the most comfortable position she could find.

The most galling part of it all was knowing he'd been right. If she'd simply given up after that mad dash round the field, it would have been tantamount to giving in and accepting defeat. She might never have found the courage to ride the mare again. As it was, she still hadn't rediscovered the old easiness and unthinking confidence she'd had as a child, but at least the numbing feeling of panic had abated.

She glowered into the darkness. Of all the people she didn't want to feel beholden to, Jamie Oliver sat squarely at the top of the list. He'd been surprisingly helpful, considerate even, but that didn't change the fact that he didn't like her, or trust her, one little bit. Well, it was mutual, she told herself moodily. She didn't like him either, the big arrogant lunk. And yet there had been moments— fleeting seconds, really—when the look in his eyes hinted at another side to the man. A side Lisa doubtless knew well, for she clearly thought the sun rose and set with him. A side that changed him from a sarcastic, autocratic chauvinist into a warm, compassionate human being. A side Casey would probably never be allowed to see properly, for he'd clearly made up his mind about her, and nothing seemed destined to change it.

The realisation gave her a tiny pang of loss, though she knew that was ridiculous. How could she lose something she'd never had in the first place? But why did he dislike her so? Try as she might to shut the whole thing out of her mind, it was the question she kept coming back to, time after time. It couldn't simply be that she had chosen to live in the country, surely? Lots of people did that. He couldn't dislike all of them—could he?

She rolled over to lie on her stomach, remembering Lisa's hint that Casey reminded Jamie of someone else. At the time she hadn't paid much attention, but now the older woman's words returned, echoing in her tired mind. Who was that someone else—a former girlfriend?

Finding no ease, she returned to lying on her back, after thumping the blameless pillows irritably. At this rate she'd be a wreck by morning. It was none of her business anyway, she reminded herself forcibly, and furthermore, there was no reason for her to care. Jamie Oliver's past was entirely his own concern—and, frankly, he was welcome to keep it that way.

CHAPTER THREE

CASEY laid down the phone with a sigh, frowning slightly as she caught sight of her own reflection in the mirror above the hall table. Right now, with her face scrubbed clean of make-up and her hair still flattened after being confined under her hard riding hat, she looked like a teenager. A disgruntled one at that, she thought with a touch of wry humour, but little wonder after that telephone conversation with Megan. It was ridiculous, perhaps, but her older sister had always had the power to make her squirm in her shoes like a rebellious schoolgirl.

It had been her seventh phone call in less than three weeks, but the subject was always the same: Fantasy. For some reason best known to herself, Megan seemed to be taking it as a personal affront that Casey had bought the mare—and she'd been even more indignant to discover she hadn't yet "come to her senses" and sold the animal on.

'I suppose it's that blasted vet's fault,' she'd said grimly tonight. 'He's to blame for this—probably trying to convince you you're going to be the next Virginia Leng. All he wants is a new client for his list, you mark my words.'

Since the words she had been instructed to mark were so clearly way off target, Casey almost began to giggle, but stifled her amusement, knowing it would only add fuel to the fire.

'Quite the opposite, actually,' she said evenly. 'Mr Oliver would probably be highly delighted if I told him I wanted to sell Fantasy. He's convinced she's just some sort of craze for me.'

'Then he's considerably more sensible than I've been giving him credit for,' Megan crowed, and Casey mentally kicked herself. There was no need to hand her sister ammunition on a plate.

'You're both wrong,' she said stiffly. 'Fantasy is important to me—and I have no intention of giving her up for anyone.'

'Sweetheart,' Megan's voice became softer, almost coaxing, 'don't you realise what you're doing? You're using the poor creature as a substitute, and that's really not fair to her, is it?'

'Substitute?' Casey's eyes narrowed. 'Just what do you mean by that?'

'Surely it's obvious? You failed in London and you lost Jody. Now you're trying to fill in the empty spaces in your life with the horse. It's understandable, but——'

'I did not fail in London,' Casey said through gritted teeth, anger hardening like a tight knot in her chest. 'I discovered I didn't like the place, so I left. I don't accept that as a failure—in fact I'd say it was a triumph—the triumph of good common sense.'

'But perhaps you wouldn't have disliked it as much if things had worked out between you and Jody.'

Casey pressed her fingers against her forehead, the strain of the conversation beginning to make her head ache. Sometimes she wondered why she ever bothered trying to get through to her indomitable older sister. It was like trying to break down a brick wall with a feather pillow.

'Look,' she said patiently, 'for the millionth time, my decision to leave London and Jody was made for positive reasons, not negative ones as you seem determined to believe. And in any case, it is *my* life—it's up to me what I do with it, surely?'

'But you have responsibilities.' Megan's voice grew solemn, and Casey dug her knuckles into her brow, knowing what was coming next. It was a record Megan had played many times before.

'When Mum and Dad died I honoured my responsibility by bringing you up the best way I knew how.' She paused as if waiting for a response, but Casey remained silent. 'Your duty is to become all that you possibly can be—to become someone they'd have been proud of.'

Her words flowed on, but Casey had stopped listening. Not that she was immune, but any means—even though intellectually she recognised Megan's tactics, emotionally she fell for them every time. It was the means by which Megan had, to a large extent, controlled and directed Casey's life. Running away from London and Jody had been one of the few major things she had done entirely of her own volition, she realised now, horrified by the sudden revelation of her own apparent weakness.

'Look, Meg,' she cut ruthlessly in to her sister's never-ending monologue, 'I really must go now. I've got important things to do.'

'At this time of night?' Megan's voice rose querulously.

'The laundry,' Casey improvised hastily. 'Late evenings are the only time I get to do the household tasks.'

'Yet you always seem to have time for the horse,' Megan gave an exasperated sigh. 'Really, Casey, you must start getting your priorities in order!'

As far as she was concerned, her priorities were in exactly the right order, Casey thought, deciding she might as well make truth out of a lie and tackle the overflowing washing basket. So long as her home was clean and in a reasonably respectable state, she wasn't about to lose any sleep over a speck of dust, or a blouse left unironed. On the other hand, her relationship with Fantasy was becoming a source of real joy. The two were already beginning to work together as a partnership, and, although she still wasn't a hundred per cent confident, Casey was becoming very much more relaxed and at ease in the saddle.

Unfortunately, the same could not be said for her relationship with Jamie Oliver. He remained an enigma—and an inconsistent one at that. Within the space of a couple of hours he could be everything from pleasant to brusque to downright insulting. Admittedly, it wasn't exactly easy to develop a rapport when she was careering round the field on a silvery grey mare, and he was standing in the centre shouting out instructions, but by the end of what had been a pretty intensive three weeks she should at least have been able to say with some conviction whether she liked him or not.

But that was the odd thing, Casey thought ruefully, transferring armfuls of clothes from the Ali

Baba basket to the washing-machine—she honestly couldn't make up her mind. She certainly looked forward to the riding lessons—in fact, they were fast becoming the highlight of the day, but that was due purely to the man's teaching skills and the delightful discovery that Fantasy was actually great fun.

Truth to tell, she didn't really know how he felt about her either. He'd certainly mellowed towards her—or perhaps he'd simply decided to be a little nicer for the sake of peaceful, harmonious lessons. Whatever—there hadn't been a repeat of the angry, hot-tempered words they'd flung at each other on their first meetings. Nor had he made any attempt again to kiss her, or even touch her, and she'd told herself more than once she should be resoundingly grateful for that. And yet, if she were to be painfully honest with herself, she would have to admit he had her well and truly intrigued. She had never met anyone quite like him before, and the simple fact that she could never quite 'get a handle on him', as Peter Brook would say, made him an endless source of fascination.

He'd accused her of pinning labels on people before she'd even met them, but he didn't fit snugly within any of the descriptions she'd mentally have compiled to fit a vet. He was all the things he should be—capable, strong, confident—but he was a whole lot of other things beside. It made her wonder if she'd ever be able to claim that she really knew him.

With that came a further realisation—a couple of weeks ago she would have sworn with complete honesty that she'd be happy never to see the man again. But somehow he'd managed to carve a place for himself in her life, even though she wasn't at all sure just what that place amounted to. She knew she'd miss him if he decided to up and leave, but surely that was simply because of all the help he'd given her with Fantasy?

She paused in the middle of unloading the spin-dried clothes, teased by the riddle of it all—they'd been together almost every evening for the past three weeks, yet she wasn't even sure if she could call him a friend.

Suddenly exasperated by it all, Casey shook her head, impatient with her own muddled thoughts. It was ridiculous to spend so much time soul-searching. Jamie Oliver certainly wouldn't.

Next evening she was just changing into her riding clothes when she heard the vet's familiar voice calling to her from the kitchen.

'I'm here.' She half ran, half stumbled through from the bedroom, trying to haul on one skin-tight leather boot en route. 'You're a little early, aren't you?'

'I'm afraid there won't be a lesson tonight.' He put out one hand to steady her, grinning at the undoubtedly comical figure she cut.

'Oh?' Casey was startled by the sharpness of the disappointment.

'Lisa called me on the car phone just as I was heading over here. One of her dogs is in labour, and having a hard time, by the sound of it. I promised I'd go straight there.'

'Can I come?' The question was out before Casey even had time to gather her thoughts.

He looked surprised. 'It can be a messy business, you know. Puppies aren't adorable little bundles of fluff immediately.'

She grinned. 'I do know. I had a Labrador once—and I was there when she gave birth. It was one of the loveliest things I'd ever seen.' She saw him hesitate and pushed the moment of advantage. 'I won't get in the way, I promise.'

He gave a curt little nod. 'Be sure you don't. Come on, then, I don't want to keep Lisa waiting.'

Lisa met them at the entrance to her yard, barely waiting for James to cut the engine before she yanked open the car door.

'Thank God you're here! I've been so worried—it's Cally's first litter and she's having a hard time. I just didn't know what to do.'

'You can calm down for a start and take us to Cally,' said Jamie with cool authority. 'Everything will be OK.'

Casey said nothing as he laid a comforting hand on the other woman's shoulder. Lisa didn't appear to have noticed she was there, her usual placid nature shot to pieces through concern for her dog.

'Where's Joe?' Jamie asked as Lisa led the way to a small utility-room off the kitchen where a bed had been made up for Cally.

Lisa gave him a ghost of her usual broad smile. 'Gone out. He knew you were coming, so she'd be in good hands, but he couldn't take any more of Cally's whining. Said it was tearing him in two.'

'And that's the man who helps bring hundreds of

lambs into the world every year without turning a hair.' Jamie chuckled. 'Lord knows how he'll cope if you two ever get round to having kids of your own.'

'I doubt he'd be any worse,' Lisa said simply, pushing a tangled strand of hair back from her strained face. 'The dogs are his life.' She knelt down at the side of the basket, crooning softly to the black and white Border collie lying panting on its side. 'Do something, Jamie! I hate to see her like this.'

He placed his hands on her shoulders and carefully lifted her to her feet. 'There's not enough room in here for all of us,' he said gently. 'Why don't you go and put the kettle on?'

'You need boiling water?'

He smiled. 'I need a cup of tea. Now go on, scoot!' As Lisa scurried away, he winked conspiratorially at Casey. 'Had to get her out of the way,' he said. 'Normally she's a great assistant, but when her own animals are concerned she goes all to pieces.'

He hunkered down beside the basket, laying a tender hand on the collie's head as she looked up at him, her soft brown eyes anxious.

'Look at that,' he said softly. 'She's in a lot of pain, yet she's wise enough to trust me. Many a human wouldn't be as wise.'

'Perhaps she knows you would never hurt her.' The words caught in Casey's throat as she watched him tend to the dog, his hands careful and quiet as he carried out his examination.

'I think the first pup's somehow become jammed,' he said at last, speaking more to himself than Casey.

'Can you help her?'

'Stroke her head for me. Just keep her distracted for a moment.' When Casey hesitated, he sent her a hard, impatient glance. 'You needn't worry—this little girl would never bite, no matter how much pain she was in.'

Casey began to tell him she wasn't afraid of being bitten, simply of accidentally doing something to hurt Cally even more, but the look on his face silenced her. He had more important things to do right now than listen to excuses. She bent over, sliding one hand under Cally's head, stroking the silky ears and murmuring soft words of instinctive comfort. As Jamie worked, the dog's eyes glazed over with pain, and Casey felt her own eyes fill with tears. She lost track of time as she sat there, trying to will away some of Cally's pain, wishing there were more she could do to help. Then Jamie gave a satisfied little grunt and she looked up, a beaming smile lighting her features as she spotted a tiny wriggling shape lying in his hands.

'You did it! Jamie, you really did it!'

Cally nosed her gently out of the way, eager for her first sight of her own new pup, and Jamie watched closely as she began licking the tiny creature.

'She'll be all right now,' he murmured. 'That first pup was just a bit on the big side.'

'It's so beautiful.' Casey couldn't tear her eyes away from the scene. 'And she's such a proud mother.'

'She'll have a lot more to be proud of before the

evening's over.' Jamie grinned, his own pleasure undisguised. 'Let's go tell Lisa the good news.'

'Can I stay?' She looked up as he got to his feet, her sherry-coloured eyes imploring. 'I'd love to see the others being born.'

He hesitated, his expression wondering as he gazed down at her. 'The television cameras should see you like this,' he said unexpectedly. 'You look far lovelier now than I've ever seen you look on screen.' Then he was gone, calling triumphantly for Lisa as Casey rocked back on her heels, stunned by what he'd said. He hadn't touched her, yet his words had been like a physical caress, bringing something deep within to tentative life. It was as if he'd lit a candle in the hidden darkness of her soul, warming a part of her she had thought forever frozen.

There was a celebration in Lisa's house that evening, Joe insisting on his return that Casey and the vet drink a toast 'to wet the babies heads'. 'An old Cumbrian custom,' he declared solemnly, his nut-brown eyes twinkling in weatherbeaten cheeks. 'Can't allow new life to arrive without welcoming it properly.'

'What he really means is that any excuse is good enough for a party,' Jamie returned, nevertheless holding out his glass for a refill. 'Watch those Cumbrian drinks, Casey, they bear no relation to regulation measures.'

Casey had taken only a couple of sips, but as Jamie smiled down at her, his dark eyes warm, she wondered if it was just the alcohol that was going to her head, making her feel giddy.

'I'm sorry we had to call you out when it's not your evening on duty,' Joe said. 'But you know Lisa—thinks no one else is good enough for her dogs——'

'Well, I like that!' Lisa cut in good-humouredly, pausing on her way back to the scullery to see the pups again. 'You were the one who insisted I call Jamie on his car phone.'

'Peace, children!' Jamie held up one imperious hand. 'Desist squabbling this second! You know I'm always happy to come out whether I'm officially on duty or not.'

'Who's been doing night-call duty over the past few weeks?' asked Casey, thinking of all the evenings he'd spent in her company and feeling a little guilty. Had she been keeping him away from his patients?

'A student on attachment from the veterinary college,' Jamie explained, chuckling at the look in her eyes. 'Don't worry, I haven't been letting a rank amateur loose among the animals—she's almost qualified and very capable.'

'Is that the young blonde lass I've seen travelling with you in the car?' Joe asked archly. 'Will she be joining you in the practice?'

Jamie quirked a rakish eyebrow. 'I rather hope so,' he drawled lazily. 'She's brightened up the place considerably. I've even had the farmers coming in to pay their bills ahead of time just to get a look at her.'

'Good grief, she must be a stunner!'

Casey laughed along with the two men, but deep inside she was cut to ribbons by shards of completely unexpected jealousy. There was no mistaking the look in Jamie's eyes when he talked about the young vet—a mixture of respect, admiration, affection— all things she'd never seen in his eyes when he looked at her, and the realisation ate into her like acid. Her cheeks began to ache with the strain of keeping a fixed smile in place as the light-hearted banter flowed around her. No wonder Jamie had been able to spend so many evenings with her—the person he really wanted to be with had been busy working.

The thought of him with the pretty blonde she'd never even met stabbed her like a knife, and she was horrified to discover just how much it hurt.

'I hope you'll all forgive me.' Suddenly she was unable to take any more. 'I should really get home now.' She rose to her feet abruptly, not meeting Jamie's eyes.

'Won't you have another drink?' Joe was clearly surprised. 'It's still early.'

She shook her head, summoning up a smile that didn't quite make it to her eyes. 'It's been a long day, and I'm tired.'

Joe snorted derisively. 'City folk! Can't cope with a bit of hard graft!'

'Leave the lass alone.' Lisa caught the end of his remark as she returned from the scullery. 'She is looking a bit weary.'

Jamie downed his whisky in one swallow and stood up, laying a hand on her shoulder. 'Come on, then. I'll drive you home.'

Casey flinched away from the contact. 'There's no

need,' she said stiffly. 'It's a short walk. I could do with some fresh air.'

'Nonsense!' He ruffled her hair in a casually friendly manner. 'I always make sure my assistants are escorted home.' The dark eyes twinkled. 'Unless they're male, of course, in which case they can fend for themselves.'

Turning away, Casey walked quickly through to the utility-room to take a last look at the pups, six squirming little bundles all wriggling close to their mother. The sight brought the sting of tears to her eyes—it was all so simple and uncomplicated. If only her own life could be as straightforward, she thought bleakly.

'Ready?'

She turned to see Jamie standing behind her, and nodded wordlessly. But when she made to walk past him, he caught her by one arm, his other hand tipping her chin upwards to face him.

'Are you crying?'

'No.'

'Then why are your eyelashes wet?'

She dashed one hand angrily over her eyes, annoyed that he'd witnessed her moment of weakness. 'It's just the puppies,' she muttered. 'Baby animals always get to me this way.'

Long, lean fingers tenderly stroked her cheek, wiping away a stray tear. 'Don't be ashamed to cry,' he said softly, and not for anything could she have torn her eyes free of his magnetic gaze. 'I've seen many animals born, but it still affects me too.'

His words were almost enough to unleash the torrent of emotion building up inside her. The

temptation to lay her head against his broad, powerful chest and simply let the tears flow was all but
overwhelming, though she couldn't really have
explained the reasons for such wrenching sorrow,
even to herself. Instead she stepped backwards,
twisting away from the warmth of his fingers, her
face deliberately void of expression as she stared up
at him.

'Perhaps you'd take me home now.'

He let his hand drop slowly back to his side, and
in his eyes she caught a flicker of disappointment,
as though she'd somehow let him down.

The journey home was a short one, but seemed
to take forever. Jamie was perfectly relaxed, hum-
ming softly under his breath as he drove, but Casey
was taut as a violin string. She found herself watching his hands on the steering-wheel, his fingers long
and capable, the nails short and workmanlike. They
were strong hands, masculine hands, hands you
could entrust your life to. But not your heart. The
thought echoed so strongly in her mind it was as if
the words had been spoken aloud, and unthinkingly
she glanced at Jamie, half afraid he'd heard them.

'Well?'

The single word hung in the air as he drew to a
halt in the farm courtyard.

'Well?' She stared at him uncomprehendingly.
'Well what?'

'Well—aren't you going to invite me in for
coffee?' It was obvious from his wide grin that he
had recovered his earlier good humour.

For a second she hesitated, tempted, then she

remembered the blonde vet and unconsciously stiffened her spine. Not for anything would she allow
herself to become just one of a string, no matter
how compelling his dark eyes.

'Sorry,' she said with forced brightness, 'I've
already told you, I'm feeling rather tired tonight.'
She gave him a patently false smile. 'Must be the
Cumbrian drinks—too much for a city girl like me.'

'Hope they don't prove too much for Mandy,
then.' His voice was clearly amused.

'Mandy?'

He nodded. 'The beautiful blonde vet. Lisa
obviously hasn't told Joe, but she's invited Mandy
down to dinner on her first night off. Typical of
Lisa—she always likes to take newcomers under her
wing.'

'I'm sure you'll be able to protect her from Joe's
drinks.' Casey forced the words past a constricted
throat, feeling a slab of misery settle in her chest.
She'd been right—his relationship with the student
vet extended beyond the professional.

'I will?' He looked puzzled. 'But I won't even be
there.'

Casey nodded dully. 'I'd forgotten. I suppose you
couldn't both take the same evening off.'

He reached over and placed his fngers along her
cheek, gently turning her to look at him. 'Mandy
wouldn't be too pleased to find her boss intruding
on a social evening,' he said carefully. 'Especially
when her fiancé will be there.'

'Her fiancé?'

He nodded. 'Nice young man—he has a farm just

a few miles from here. That's why she wanted to come to our practice for her attachment.'

Casey looked down at her hands, clenched in her lap, gripped by a mixture of emotions, not sure whether she should laugh or cry. Then Jamie leaned over to unfasten her seatbelt, and the jolt of sheer joy rushing through her system nearly unmanned her enough to give in to the severe temptation to tangle her fingers in his dark unruly hair. Only will-power kept her rigidly still, and she wondered hazily just what it was about this man that made her so want to reach out to him. With Jody, in the early days at least, she had shared an easy, laughing companionship. It hadn't been difficult to touch him—he had always been happy to hold hands or walk along with a friendly arm warm about her shoulders. But with Jamie it was different—instinctively she knew that touching him might unleash something within herself she would have no control over.

'Are you all right?' His face was just a matter of inches from her own, and she swallowed hard, unable to drag her eyes from his mouth—a mouth that could only have been carved by the hand of a master sculptor. Those lips had touched hers once, and the longing to taste them again in all their plundering glory made her tremble.

'Just fine,' she managed breathlessly. 'I felt a little dizzy for a moment. Must be——'

'The Cumbrian drinks—yes, I know.' Gently he touched her hair, and the light contact sent a dart of heat rushing through her veins. 'Off you go now and get to bed. I'd hate to have your make-up lady

chasing me to complain about dark circles under
your eyes!'

For a heart-stopping moment she thought he was
about to kiss her, and every fibre in her body
seemed to clamour for his touch. Instead he simply
smiled and gave her a tiny push.

'Go on, Casey, I'll see you tomorrow.'

The farmhouse was quiet when she let herself in,
and she found herself missing the happy, noisy
warmth of Lisa's disorganised home. If she were
honest with herself, she envied Lisa her relationship
with Joe, which was made stronger still when out-
siders were allowed in. She'd once thought she could
have that kind of relationship with Jody. When he
insisted she go to London with him, she had visualised setting up a warm, inviting home with him,
where laughter would ring out frequently and
friends would always be assured of a welcome.
Instead he'd seen their tiny flat merely as a place to
store his clothes and sleep in, preferring to do his
socialising in the city's vast array of wine bars and
nightclubs.

At first she had tagged along with him, but she'd
never really felt at home in the increasingly high-
powered circles he found so irresistible. That had
been the real problem between them, she acknowledged ruefully, pouring a cup of coffee to take to
bed. Their dreams had always been different, but
they'd been blinded to that by the old bonds that
had tied them together since they were teenagers.

In his way, Jody had needed her there. For all his
apparent arrogance, there was a vulnerability to him
that perhaps only she recognised, probably because

she'd been there in the sometimes painful days of his youth, a constant ally and support.

For the first time she found herself questioning her feelings for Jamie Oliver—after her reactions tonight, there was no way she could go on fooling herself that she wasn't attracted to him in some way. But why should she hunger now for a man she hadn't even liked at first? Could it simply be his unquestionable strength—was she just searching for another dominant character to lead her along by the nose?

The thought continued to plague her as she slid beneath the covers, and it stayed with her throughout a long and restless night.

CHAPTER FOUR

'ARE you OK, Casey love? You look ready to keel over in a heap.'

'What?' Casey looked up into a pair of concerned brown eyes. 'I'm sorry, Blake, what did you say? I was miles away.'

Blake Johnstone turned from the sound-mixing desk to look at her properly. 'On another planet, I'd say.' He frowned worriedly, taking in her pallor, and the heaviness of her sherry-coloured eyes. 'You don't look at all well,' he said frankly. 'Not that I'm surprised, after spending four solid days in this glorified cupboard.'

Casey smiled, appreciating the film editor's concern. 'You're in here all day every day,' she reminded him, nodding towards the two TV screens and mixing desks which dominated the editing suite.

'Ah, but I'm accustomed to it.' Blake nodded sagely. 'You, on the other hand, are used to flying about the countryside, doing news stories here, there and everywhere, not sitting about for hours on end gazing at pictures on a screen.'

'Such are the joys of putting together a half-hour programme.' She tried to shrug off his concern, but Blake wasn't having any of it.

'It's not just that,' he said abruptly. 'You look as if you might have caught a bug—flu, maybe.'

Casey smiled faintly. 'Just a headache,' she said,

61

omitting to mention that a little drummer boy had been pounding a steady beat in her temples since early that morning. 'Anyway, I can't have flu—this is summer!'

Blake shook his head. 'Germs love mild weather—lets them breed in comfort.' He eyed her consideringly for a moment, then stood up and gently pulled her to her feet. 'Come on, love—you look dead on your feet. You're going home.'

'But I can't! What about the editing?'

'Almost finished, as you well know. Anyway, I know what you want for the last couple of minutes—you can trust me to do it as you want.'

'Are you sure?' Casey felt herself weakening as he hefted the strap of her bag on to her shoulder. She had been feeling pretty miserable all morning.

'I'm positive.' Blake patted her shoulder. 'Anyway, I can always phone you if I have problems. Now go on, I'll clear things with Peter. OK?'

She gave in with a smile. 'OK.'

By the time she reached home she was feeling decidedly groggy. With an effort she dragged herself to the field to check on Fantasy, smiling ruefully as she watched the silvery grey mare enjoy a luxurious roll in a patch of deep green grass. 'I'll come out and see you later,' she called, wincing as the effort hurt her throat. 'But this evening it'll be just you and me, so you'd better be on your best behaviour.' She turned away with a sigh, depression weighing as heavily as the decision she'd reached somewhere in the course of a restless, feverish night.

Somehow she had to break the pattern of weak compliance she had fallen into over the years almost without realising it—and the first step towards that would be telling Jamie Oliver politely but firmly that his services as a riding instructor were no longer required.

Heading towards the farmhouse, she groaned heavily. Even now she wasn't being completely honest with herself. Getting Jamie out of her life might prove she was strong enough to make her own decisions, but it was also going to hurt like hell. But if she didn't do it now, the pain could be positively crucifying later.

Almost without her realising it, he had become important in her life—seeing him, the most important part of every day. She hadn't been fully aware of that until the thought of another woman in his life had all but paralysed her with jealousy. OK, so she'd been mistaken about the blonde vet, but that had simply brought home to her just how vulnerable she was becoming where he was concerned. For the sake of her own emotional survival, she couldn't afford to become any more involved with someone who saw her at best as a riding pupil, at worst as an ambition-ridden city kid playing at being a country girl.

She stumbled wearily towards the bedroom, feeling as though every muscle in her body had begun to ache in throbbing unison. Taking off her clothes seemed too much like hard work, so she settled for kicking off her shoes, then simply toppled over on to the welcoming mattress, hugging a pillow to her forehead.

'Just a little nap,' she whispered. 'Then I'll face Jamie and tell him I don't need him any more.'

Several hours later she drited back to consciousness, hazily aware that things weren't quite as they should be, but unable to pin-point the change. Suddenly the penny dropped and she sat bolt upright, groaning as the abrupt movement set her head thumping.

'Careful, sweetheart.' Jamie Oliver's low tones washed over her like a soothing ointment. 'You're not well, you need to rest.'

'I'm in bed.' She glared at him accusingly.

He laid a cool hand against her hot forehead. 'Very good, Casey,' he said with a faint grin. 'You're fevered, but obviously not delirious if you can reach such complicated conclusions.'

'No—I mean I'm *in* bed,' Casey said again, forcing the words past a painfully raw throat. 'And I'm wearing a shirt. One that doesn't even belong to me.'

'Top marks.' He sat down on the bed and gently pushed her back against the pillows. 'I did look for a nightdress, but none of those frilly little numbers really seemed quite the thing for someone in her sickbed.' He grinned wickedly. 'Though the thought of seeing you wearing one of them was decidedly tempting, I confess.'

The idea of him rummaging through her lingerie drawer to find a nightdress would have made her blush scarlet had her cheeks not already been flushed with fever.

'What's going on here?' she asked weakly, giving up the struggle to make sense of the situation. 'I don't understand.'

'Poor little girl!' His dark eyes were compassionate as he caught her wrist and expertly located her
pulse. 'You really are feeling awful, aren't you?'

She nodded dolefully and he laughed softly.
'Don't worry, it's only a flu bug—there's a lot of it
about just now. Joe's feeling pretty poorly today as
well.'

'But how did I get into bed? And where did this
shirt come from?'

'From my car,' Jamie explained. 'Vets have to do
some pretty mucky jobs sometimes, so I usually
carry a spare set of clothes.'

Casey fingered the soft cotton of the shirt for a
moment, embarrassment mounting as realisation
slowly dawned.

'How did I get the shirt on?' she croaked at last,
not at all sure she wanted to hear the answer.

He tilted her chin upward. 'When I arrived you
were totally out for the count,' he murmured. 'So
much so that I couldn't get a word of sense out of
you—you kept mumbling about Fantasy, and telling
me you weren't really weak, just flexible.' He eyed
her curiously. 'What was that all about?'

She stared back mutely, unable to find words to
explain.

He shrugged. 'Not to worry, I'll get to the bottom
of that one later, when you're feeling better.
Anyway—since you were obviously in no fit state to
fend for yourself, I put you to bed. You haven't
stirred in hours.'

Casy caught sight of the clothes she'd been wearing earlier, neatly folded over a chair, and groaned
despairingly. 'You undressed me?'

He nodded. 'Don't worry about it—I'm a medical man, remember?' A mischievous smile played about his lips. 'Though I must say, that was a much more pleasant task than many I'm called upon to undertake in the course of duty.'

She dropped her face into her hands, unable to meet his knowing eyes any longer.

'Sweetheart, don't be embarrassed. You were sick—I'd have done the same for anyone in the same position.'

'Thanks,' she said dully, his reassuring words making her feel even worse. Then a thought occurred to her and she glanced up quickly, her own predicament forgotten.

'Fantasy! I haven't seen to her.'

'But I have.' He caught her hands. 'Don't worry, she's fine. I'll look after her till you're well again.'

'I can't possibly ask you to——'

'You haven't asked me,' he cut in firmly, laying one finger on her lips to stay her protest. 'I've offered. And it's no trouble at all.'

'I suppose this will just convince you all the more that I'm not capable of looking after her,' Casey muttered unhappily.

'On the contrary, I think you've done a pretty good job for a beginner. And, after all, anyone can fall sick.' He stood up. 'Now, I want you to get some rest. I won't be far away, so just call out if you need anything.'

'You don't need to stay. Really, I'll be fine.' An enormous sneeze prevented her from saying any more, and she groped miserably for a tissue.

He sighed exasperatedly. 'Suffering an attack of

independence again? Look, Casey, why don't you just accept the fact that you're sick and need a little help from your friends? It can happen to the best of us, you know.' He sent her a mock-stern glance. 'Now, I'm going to put the light out, young lady, so get some sleep. Rest's the thing for you right now.'

She subsided back against the pillows, too worn out to argue further. Then she remembered that Jamie had undressed her as she lay unconscious, blissfully unaware, and the thought drove her further beneath the covers as though she could escape it that way. She had always been shy of displaying her body. Even on the beach when other women boldly flaunted themselves in states of near nudity, she stuck to the kind of costume she had worn as a schoolgirl: practical and functional, and revealing as little as possible. It wasn't that she was unduly prudish, she reasoned, simply that she didn't consider her boyishly slim body worth showing off.

Now Jamie Oliver had seen for himself what she normally kept modestly hidden, and the thought depressed her unutterably. It was ridiculous in any case, she told herself angrily—someone as vitally masculine as Jamie must inevitably be attracted to an equally feminine woman. In comparison she was built like an immature schoolgirl.

Her dreams that night, made more vivid than normal by her illness, saw her standing on the shoreline of a crowded beach. Just a few yards away stood Jamie, but though she was calling out to him he appeared not to have noticed her, so entranced was he by a long parade of blonde beauties shimmying past him like Miss World contestants, each one more buxom than the last.

As they disappeared, Jamie turned slowly to face her, and began to laugh, a harsh sound that cut into her like knives. She glanced downward, realising to her horror that she was stark naked. She turned away, trying to run into the concealing waves, but the sand became like a bog, sucking her down, snaring her in its grasp. As she went under all she could hear was cold, cruel laughter ringing in the air.

She awoke covered in sweat and struggling against the imprisoning sand, only to find herself beating wildly against a broad, immovable chest.

'Hush, hush, little one,' Jamie's voice crooning softly into her hair finally got through her addled senses and she stopped struggling, slumping exhaustedly against him as hot tears began to flow.

'I'm sorry,' she gasped brokenly. 'It was just a bad dream. I don't know what's wrong with me— I'm not usually as pathetic as this.'

'Stop apologising, silly girl.' The reprimand was gentle. 'You had a nightmare because you're sick— it's quite common. Want to tell me about it?'

She shook her head. Describing the dream would be far too revealing—would tell him more about her feelings than she ever wanted him to know.

'I'll be fine,' she said, her voice muffled against his chest.

'Nevertheless, I think I'll stay here, at least until you fall asleep again.' He grinned. 'Hearing you scream out like that must have taken about ten years off my life. I nearly hit the roof!'

'I'm sorry.' Unconsciously Casey let her fingers

trail over his chest, feeling the thick pelt of hair beneath the thin cotton of his shirt.

He drew in his breath sharply. 'And you'd better stop doing that, or I'm liable to hit the roof again, but for a very different reason.' He trapped her wandering fingers with one hand. 'Go back to sleep, minx. And don't worry, I'll keep the bad dreams away.'

Comforted by his presence, and the warm strength of the arms holding her close, Casey stopped fighting sleep and gave in gracefully, snuggling closer to him as conscious thought fled.

It took a full week for Casey to throw off the flu bug that had felled her at the knees so unexpectedly. And during that week, Jamie Oliver seemed hardly ever to be away from her side. He was there when she woke in the morning, his wide, surprisingly boyish grin the first thing she saw on opening her eyes. He was there to bully her gently into eating the light meals Lisa sent up at regular intervals 'for the invalid', and he was there to catch her when she tried to get up too soon and all but keeled over from the effort.

'Don't push yourself so hard, sweetheart,' he admonished her gently, tucking the covers about her as though she were a child. 'It's no sin to be a little weak when you're ill.'

But that was just the trouble, she thought resentfully, watching his broad back as he strode from the room—the last thing she wanted him to think her was weak. It was bad enough that Megan and Jody regarded her as some sort of spineless pushover, but to know that Jamie had seen her at her most helpless was galling in the extreme. He'd been wonderful, there could be no denying that. Tending to her had brought out a warmth and compassion in him she would never have suspected existed if she hadn't seen him ministering to Lisa's dog Cally.

She turned over in bed with a disgusted snort. That was all she really was to him—just another patient, albeit a rather unusual one. When he returned to the room she was lying on her side gazing moodily towards the window, her eyebrows drawn together in a scowl.

'You really don't have to spend so much time with me, you know. I'm not likely to expire just because you're not here.' Even to her own ears the words sounded surly and ungracious, and she bit her lip, annoyed at herself. To her surprise he sent her a quick flashing grin, obviously unconcerned by her mood.

'Feeling grouchy, are we? That's a good sign.'

'A good sign?' Her eyes flickered curiously towards him.

He nodded. 'Means you're getting better.'

'Why?'

He sat down on the bed beside her and she resisted the urge to move closer to him. Weak she might be, but she wasn't about to hand herself over like a gift-wrapped present.

'Haven't you heard the old saying "when the devil is sick, the devil a saint will be"? Well, you're fast losing your claim to sainthood, so I reckon it must follow that you're on the mend.'

'If anyone deserves a halo round here, it should

be you,' she said solemnly, feeling faintly ashamed
of her earlier bad temper. 'I realise you've spent
practically all of your spare time here looking after
me, and I do appreciate it. I don't suppose I've been
the world's best patient.'

'Certainly not the world's easiest, from my point
of view.' Jamie's lips curved into a self-mocking
smile. 'And I don't think you should order up my
halo just yet—believe me, I've entertained some
very unsaintlike thoughts over the past few days.'

His eyes darkened and she felt her heart quicken
perceptibly. 'What sort of thoughts?' she whispered
breathlessly, half afraid of the answer.

His eyes raked over her, and even though she was
wearing a voluminous nightdress borrowed from
Lisa she felt suddenly naked beneath his gaze.

'The sort that make me very glad I'm a vet and
not a doctor, because if any GP had the thoughts
I've been having about one of his patients he'd be
struck off the register immediately.'

He slid closer to her and she felt as though she'd
suddenly forgotten how to breathe, his nearness
making her dizzy. Unthinkingly she ran her tongue
over lips grown strangely dry.

'Seeing you lying there in that huge bed, all alone,
your glorious hair like tongues of flame on the white
pillows, your lovely skin even paler than normal,
then holding you as you slept, watching your breasts
rise and fall with your breathing—it was enough to
make any man forget the Hippocratic oath.'

'My b-breasts?' Trying to lighten the suddenly
electric atmosphere, she stumbled over the word.

'Yes, Casey.' He grasped her by the shoulders,

his eyes intent as they searched her face. 'Don't tell me you're embarrassed by the word—women should never be embarrassed by anything as lovely.'

She shook her head. 'I'm not,' she protested unconvincingly. 'It's just that I've always felt rather. . .' she hesitated, belatedly wishing she'd never got into this conversation '. . .rather lacking in that department,' she finished lamely.

'You don't seriously mean that?' Jamie shook his head incredulously. 'You forget, Casey—I've seen you naked.'

'I hadn't forgotten,' she muttered, her lashes casting shadows on her cheeks as she glanced downwards.

He cupped her face in one hand, his long fingers warm against her cheek. 'Then if you don't realise it yourself, let me tell you something, Casey—you have a beautiful body. A tiny, delicate work of art, a body that could haunt a man's mind forever after he'd seen it just once.'

She gazed at him wonderingly, his words caressing her like ribbons of silk. 'You're not serious?' she whispered.

His lips quirked into a half-smile. 'You think not? Then let me assure you, Miss Casey Connolly, journalist and television star, if I didn't think it might hamper your speedy recovery, I'd demonstrate right now just how serious I am.' His fingers traced the shape of her cheekbones, then slid beneath her hair to cup the nape of her neck and draw her closer. 'But consider this to be a statement of intent.' Before she had time to react, he was kissing her, his mouth tender but firm, brooking no argument as it raked her tender flesh, her lips opening freely to his gentle insistence. His arms closed about her and she went willingly into his embrace, her nipples stiffening as her breasts flattened against his chest. His tongue played a tantalisingly erotic game with her own, dipping, sliding, cajoling a response she could never have denied him. His hand slid down to cup one breast and she whimpered softly, the touch of his hand too exquisite to deny.

When he raised his head at last she could only gaze up at him, her eyes unfocused, cloudy with the desire he had instilled, but left unfulfilled.

'I could make love to you right now, Casey,' he murmured. 'It would be so easy to simply let go, to kiss your satin skin and caress you till you cried out for release, but it wouldn't be fair. You're still too weak.'

She stiffened, misunderstanding him. 'That's a little presumptuous, don't you think?' she ground out, willing her treacherous body to stop yearning for more of his tender assault. 'What makes you think I wanted you to?'

He smiled, glancing downwards. 'Your body makes me think you wanted me to,' he said softly, but with a masculine arrogance that made her long to strike him. 'Your words may say one thing, but these. . .' He touched her breasts gently and she flinched, seeing her nipples pushing against the thin material of the nightdress. 'They tell their own story.'

'Then they're lying,' she said sharply, catching his hand and flinging it abruptly away from her.

'Are you sure, Casey?' He was unperturbed; his eyes were still caressing as he gazed at her. 'People tell lies.' Slowly, unhurriedly, he got to his feet. 'But their bodies never do.' He walked towards the door, but looked back at the last moment. 'Don't feel annoyed because I stopped when I did,' he said. 'We've got all the time in the world.'

Then he was gone, leaving Casey glaring at a closed door, clenching her hands through sheer frustration. How dared he? Just who did he think he was, the big, arrogant swine? Had he expected her to simply fall into his lap like a ripe apple newly plucked from a tree?

She fell back against the pillows, giving vent to her feelings in a series of short but heartfelt oaths. The worst part of the whole thing was facing up to the truth of it—she would have been his for the taking, and she had been annoyed he'd stopped when he had—even more annoyed that she hadn't been the one to call a halt. At least then she wouldn't have this awful feeling that her pride had just been trampled into the ground. Dammit, why was she so weak where he was concerned? Had she no will-power at all? Ruefully she remembered her cast-iron decision to tell him she no longer wanted his help with Fantasy. That had crumbled into dust fast enough. Well, for her own sake she'd simply have to start being a great deal more ruthless—this time she'd tell him to get out of her life and really mean it.

She closed her eyes, feeling already a little of the pain the decision would bring her. But it was no good—other than Fantasy, they had nothing in common. And he didn't really want her—he'd made that clear enough from the start, with his hostile opposition to her. All he wanted was the use of her body—until someone else appeared on the horizon and he wandered off to sample other pastures new, probably leaving her without as much as a backward wave. She hadn't forgotten Lisa's tales of the hearts he'd broken in his time—but he wouldn't add hers to the list.

CHAPTER FIVE

HER decision reached, Casey worked out a plan of action for getting Jamie Oliver out of her life. After all the time he'd spent with her, helping with Fantasy, then caring for her when she was ill, it would be churlish in the extreme to simply turn round and give him his marching orders with no warning whatsoever, she reasoned. Though there was something very satisfying in the thought of sending the big lunk packing, with a few choice adjectives ringing in his ears and his tail between his legs! But she had to go about it in the most tactful manner possible, since she didn't want Lisa or anyone else in the village to think she'd been ungracious. If she was subtle enough, he probably wouldn't even realise he'd been carefully shoe-horned out of his place in Casey's existence.

With all that in mind, she spent her first full day out of bed planning and preparing for a very special dinner party—a dinner party for two during which she'd tell him she was extremely grateful for all the valiant work he'd put in on her behalf. She'd tell him—quite truthfully—that she could never have done it on her own. Then, politely but firmly, she'd tell him that from here-on-in she intended to fly solo—that it was up to her now to manage alone.

As she rehearsed the dialogue over and over in her mind, the scheme seemed perfectly feasible—

logical even. He would probably be quite relieved to be freed from a responsibility which was perhaps becoming a bit irksome. After all, a good-looking man must have better things to do with his nights than play Pony Club teacher. Casey tried to skim over that thought, but infuriatingly it was the only one that stuck, jabbing into her like a sharpened needle. To escape from it, and feeling a sudden return of the energy she'd been lacking over the past week, she set about cleaning the farmhouse, tackling the various neglected chores with a gusto that would have made even Megan proud.

Later she drove to the next village, which boasted a small supermarket, to buy provisions for the meal. Since the store didn't stock anything exotic, and since if she was any judge of character Jamie Oliver's culinary tastes ran to the simple but plentiful, she laid in enough to feed the average hungry army.

Trundling her trolley along the aisles, she halted abruptly before the tiny liquor section. Alcohol was a problem. She'd already learned on the night Cally's pups were born that Jamie wasn't averse to taking a drink or two—and she could hardly lay on a meal without including at least a bottle of wine. But, on the other hand, she definitely didn't want him to get the wrong impression. The meal was intended to be both thanks and farewell, but certainly not a cosy prelude to a seductive evening. In any case, she wasn't at all sure her own defences against him could cope with the softening influence of alcohol.

Sighing gustily, she picked up two bottles of a fairly mediocre white wine and planted them firmly on top of the other goods in the trolley. If nothing else, a couple of glasses of wine would fortify her—give her a touch of Dutch courage for the task she'd set herself.

She was just turning the corner at the end of one aisle when her trolley cannoned straight into another one and she looked up, already smiling an apology, only to find herself looking into Jamie Oliver's amused eyes.

'Well, well,' he drawled. 'What a happy coincidence! I'm glad you manage to steer Fantasy rather more accurately than you do your trolley.'

'I wasn't aware that you automatically had right of way,' she returned with a saccharine-sweet smile.

'Haven't you studied your supermarket code, Casey?' He raised a questioning eyebrow. 'Don't you know it's written in tablets of stone that in such establishments all males are to be regarded with extreme pity and perhaps even a measure of contempt—but certainly never as the equal to the female of the species. Therefore this. . .' he glanced down at the two trolleys, locked together by the front wheels '. . .this unfortunate encounter must inevitably be your fault, since no mere male could be expected to know any better.'

Unable to resist his uncharacteristic attack of silliness, she found herself laughing. 'You're right, Mr Oliver—I should have remembered that age-old lesson learned at my grandmother's knee, that all men are idiots, but never more so than in the supermarket.'

He eyed the contents of her trolley interestedly.

'Buying for something special?' he queried, picking up one of the bottles of wine and studying its label.

Casey took a deep breath. 'Well, yes, as a matter of fact.' She paused, wondering how best to word the invitation. 'I decided I wanted to thank you for all the help you've given me with Fantasy,' she said, the words coming in a rush. 'And also for the way you've looked after me while I've been ill.'

'Thank me?' There was a definite rakish gleam in his dark eyes and she began to grow unaccountably warm. 'I can suggest several ways for you to do that, if you're at all short of ideas.'

'I think we're blocking the aisles, Mr Oliver,' she returned primly, horrified by the rush of delicious adrenalin his teasingly suggestive words triggered. Leaning over, she deftly unsnagged the two wheels, all too aware that he was watching her every move, his gaze practically burning through the tight denim of her jeans as the material stretched with her bending movement.

She straightened up, trying to ignore the scarlet flush in her normally too-pale cheeks, then strode on determinedly, and he fell easily into step beside her, happily oblivious that they were now creating even more of a traffic jam in the narrow passageway.

'So what's it to be?' he queried amiably. 'Candle-lit supper for two? Wine and roses? Or were you thinking more of oysters and champagne?' His mouth quirked wickedly. 'I've heard that can be a mighty explosive combination.'

'I was thinking more along the lines of chicken Maryland and coffee,' she said starchily. 'After all, I'm just up out of my sickbed.'

'So you are,' he nodded solemnly. 'You mustn't overdo it. In fact, if I were your doctor, I'd probably prescribe an early night to round it all off.'

Only the fact that they'd reached the check-out saved him from the stinging retort that rushed to her lips. Aware that the young woman on the till was giving them a highly speculative glance, Casey paid for her groceries in tight-lipped silence. Jamie, on the other hand, favoured the girl with a huge wink as he packed his shopping haphazardly into a couple of carrier bags.

'Life can be so difficult for the single male,' he sighed dramatically. 'Everything seems to be sold in packs of two. And double beds always seem so much more comfortable than single ones.' He laid a proprietorial hand on Casey's shoulder. 'Isn't that true, Case?'

Casey threw him a horrified look and shot out of the shop as though she'd been fired from a gun, the check-out girl's giggle following her out on to the street.

'Just what was that little display intended to prove?' she hissed at Jamie as he sauntered casually after her.

'Display?' He considered the word. 'What can you mean?'

'You know perfectly well what I mean—you deliberately set that girl up to believe we were—we were——'

'We were what?' The dark blue eyes were the picture of injured innocence.

'Sleeping together!' She all but spat the words at him.

'Did I? Did I really?' He thought about that for a moment, then pursed his lips. 'Surely not? I merely passed a comment about beds—it was perfectly above board, unless of course you happen to possess a mischievous mind.' Reaching his car, he stopped and regarded her steadily. 'Do you, Casey? Possess a mischievous mind, I mean?'

'Certainly not,' she snapped. 'I——'

'Pity.' He shook his head sadly. 'It might be the saving of you.'

'The saving of me?' The curious phrase stopped her growing irritation in its tracks. 'What do you mean by that exactly?'

'I'll explain over dinner. The invitation still stands, I take it?'

Effectively painted into a corner, Casey could only nod. 'Tomorrow evening, seven-thirty sharp,' she muttered mutinously.

'Perfect.' He opened the car door and slid his long legs beneath the wheel. A thought occurred to him and he frowned. 'You aren't going back to work tomorrow, are you?'

She shook her head. 'Tomorrow's Saturday. I hardly ever have to work on Saturdays.'

His expression cleared. 'I'd forgotten that. In that case you'll have time to exercise Fantasy earlier?'

'Yes, but——'

'Good. Have her saddled up after lunchtime. I'll be there about two o'clock.'

Before she had time to protest at his autocratic commands, he'd shut the car door and was revving up the engine.

'Yes, sir, *mon capitaine*.' Casey sent a sardonic

salute after the disappearing car. Still, as she walked towards her own vehicle, she couldn't help but smile. It seemed there were many faces to Jamie Oliver, and this morning she'd been given a good look at one she'd only glimpsed before. He'd been positively playful, she thought wonderingly, a million miles removed from the stern-faced grouch she'd encountered that first evening in the stable-yard.

But why show that face to her now? Was he beginning, after all this time, to trust her—perhaps even to like her a little? Since she'd decided now was the best time to oust him from her life, his timing could only be described as truly lamentable, she thought ruefully.

There again, perhaps it was heaven-sent. She'd had a hard enough time imagining her days without the dark and moody Jamie. If she'd been allowed to really get to know that warm and infinitely appealing side of him any better, she might never have been able to let go at all.

Her cheek muscles felt slightly painful when she woke the following morning, as though she'd been frowning in her sleep. She grimaced at herself in the mirror, searching her flawless skin for any tell-tale signs, but finding none. She'd been lucky so far in escaping any lines. Not that twenty-seven was exactly decrepit, she reminded herself, but she knew others of the same age who were already beginning to gather a few give-away marks of time marching relentlessly on. If it weren't for a faint network fanning out from the corners of her eyes, she knew without fake modesty that she could still be taken for a teenager, particularly when she was dressed in riding kit with a hard hat hiding her hair.

That led her on to wondering what she should wear for the evening meal. It was sorely tempting to settle for jodhpurs, she thought mutinously, or at best a pair of jeans and a comfortable old sweatshirt. But no, the occasion did merit something more, and perhaps she'd help her own case by wearing something designed to bolster her already flagging self-confidence.

Ignoring the various household tasks still waiting to be done, she rifled quickly through her wardrobe, considering, then discarding one outfit after another. The rust-coloured suit was too formal, the grey jacket and trousers too casual, the multi-coloured dress too flamboyant, the navy-blue skirt too dull. Reaching the end of the rail without success, she gazed hopelessly at the collection of clothes, wishing she could dump the whole lot in the nearest river. There just wasn't a suitable thing in the whole damn wardrobe!

Then she remembered her first idea and snapped her fingers triumphantly. Which were the clothes she always felt most at home and at ease in? Jodhpurs, boots and a warm cotton shirt. Well, the jodhs obviously wouldn't be suitable, particularly as she'd be riding that afternoon, and didn't exactly want to smother the poor man in L'air du Cheval— but there was an alternative. Dropping to her knees, she pulled out the drawer beneath the bed and began rummaging, heedless of the clothes that had been neatly folded there.

'Eureka!' She pulled a pair of black corduroy breeches from the bottom of the drawer and held them up triumphantly. She hadn't worn them in an age, but teamed with a dashingly ruffled white cotton shirt they'd be just perfect.

Even as she visualised the outfit, she could hear Megan's pained voice echoing from the past—'Really, Cassandra, must you always dress as a boy? I'm sure people must think I have a little brother, not a sister.'

Well, what the heck? She'd been born a tomboy, and, if all Megan's efforts hadn't been able to change her, it didn't seem likely there'd be much alteration in her taste or character now. And if she was—as Megan had so often darkly predicted—'still climbing trees at ninety'—then so much the better. Better to grow old disgracefully than moulder away into querulous senility.

The smile died on her lips as she suddenly recalled the last time she had worn the breeches and the ruffled shirt. She had been with Jody at a party in London—a very sophisticated affair it had been, with the men in DJs and bow-ties, the women in off-the-shoulder taffeta numbers. In comparison she'd felt like an under-fed teenager, all legs and angles.

But tonight would be different. Tonight there would be no one to compare herself to, no female eyes to glance disparagingly in her direction. Tonight there would be just Jamie and herself, seated at opposite sides of the dining table, the soft glow of the candles sending a warm glimmer into his eyes as he reached for her hand and told her just how much she was beginning to mean to him.

Stop! Mentally she screeched to a halt, her mind slamming on its own brakes. What on earth was she doing? she admonished herself fiercely—she was supposed to be planning ways to get rid of him, not fantasising over the great lunk!

Disgusted with her own wayward mind, Casey resolutely turned to thoughts of the evening meal, and she headed for the kitchen to begin its preparations. She'd never been a terribly adventurous cook, but she was perfectly capable of turning out nice, wholesome fare. If something deep within yearned to set out just the sort of feast Jamie had teasingly suggested, she cut the thought off in its infancy.

Glancing at the clock some time later, she was horrified to see she had only half an hour left before he was due to arrive. With a cheese sandwich in one hand and a cup of coffee in the other, she went through to the bedroom, managing to eat, strip off her clothes and reach for her riding kit at the same time. Casting a harassed glance at the bedroom, she gave a rueful sigh, imagining the ticking-off she'd get if Megan were there. She had always been a stickler for tidiness, but Casey seemed always to be in too much of a rush, trying to do too many other things to bother unduly about such matters. It was only surface clutter, she reassured herself, nothing more than a few items of clothing scattered about, and a couple of books lying open on the bedside table. In any case, there was no need to panic— thanks to yesterday's rush of energy, the rest of the house was spick and span. And though he had been in her bedroom often enough while she had been ill, there was no way Jamie Oliver would be setting foot in there tonight.

She hauled a sweatshirt on, suddenly remembering his teasing remarks about beds the previous day, and as her head emerged her eyes were drawn inexorably to her own hugely comfortable double bed, with its prettily patterned blue and yellow quilt. Against her better judgement she allowed herself for just a second to imagine him lying there, and her body weakened under the onslaught of a rush of longing so intense it made her knees tremble. It was crazy, she told herself helplessly, self-destructive even, but there was something so compelling about the man that trying to free herself from his spell would be like trying to drag metal shavings from a powerful magnet.

But somehow, for the sake of her own survival, and because she knew in her heart she could never ultimately mean more to him than one of the girls he'd tumbled with so heedlessly in the hay, somehow she had to prise herself free.

Minutes later she was saddling Fantasy in the stable, apologising for the hasty brush-over that was all she'd had time to give the little mare.

'Time just ran away with me, I think,' she said, carefully tightening the girth. 'That's what comes of not being a very well organised person, I suppose.'

She was still chatting to the animal, smiling as Fantasy flicked back her ears to listen, when the sound of hoofs ringing on the flagstones of the courtyard made her stop in her tracks. Curiously she walked out of the stable, and her mouth fell open in amazement at the sight of Jamie sitting astride one of the most beautiful horses she had ever seen. Standing over sixteen hands, the bay gelding positively gleamed with health, its muscles rippling beneath skin as sleek as silk. Beside him poor little half-groomed Fantasy would look like a scruffy little seaside pony.

'Where on earth did you find him?' Astonishment made Casey less than gracious.

'Good afternoon to you too.' A muscle twitching in his left cheek betrayed Jamie's amusement. 'This is Spud. He's from the kennels in the village.'

'Spud?' Her eyebrows shot up to disappear beneath her fringe. 'Kennels?'

'The hunt kennels,' he explained with exaggerated patience. 'He's one of the hunt horses. The chief whipper-in generally rides him, but I occasionally take him out for a spot of exercise. Don't I, Spud old boy?' He fondled the animal's ears affectionately.

'Spud?' Casey knew she was beginning to sound like a cracked record, but couldn't help herself. The vision of Jamie so tall and proud on the magnificent animal seemed to have addled her brain.

'He has a much fancier name, of course, but they don't have time for all that nonsense at the kennels,' he returned with an amused grin. 'You'd never find a horse called Fantasy there, that's for sure. It would have been shortened to Fanny long since.' He eyed her curiously. 'Now are you going to bring the little lady out and mount up, or are you going to stand there looking bemused all day? We're wasting good riding time.'

Despite her own confusion, Casey couldn't help but giggle at Fantasy's expression of pure astonishment when she caught sight of the debonair Spud.

'I know, sweetheart,' Casey murmured softly as the mare gave the gelding a long amorous look. 'He is a stunner. But don't you be taken in by looks alone. He could be a rogue underneath that suave exterior.'

'Sounds as though the lady's speaking from experience,' Jamie ventured casually, leaning down to check his girth.

'Or simply common sense,' Casey retorted sharply. She put one foot in the stirrup and found herself hopping around as Fantasy began to sidle closer to the bay. 'Don't be such a flirt, girl! Let him come to you.'

'Another piece of wisdom learned the hard way?' Jamie said drily. 'Don't let her get away with that, Casey, make her stand still till you're properly settled in the saddle and ready to move off.'

'Easier said than done!' Red-faced with a mixture of embarrassment and exertion, she tightened her hold on the reins and spoke sharply to the mare. 'She's excited because Spud's here, that's all.'

'Of course she is, but you mustn't let her forget her manners, especially in company. Be firm with her, Casey, kind but firm. She'll like you all the better for it in the long run.'

'Now who's speaking from experience?' Casey shot him a telling look as she finally mounted up. 'Is that the secret of your legendary success with women?'

He favoured her with a flashing grin, his eyes twinkling with undeniable devilment. 'Legendary? I wouldn't have rated myself quite as highly, Miss Connolly. Who have you been talking to?'

She gave an audible sniff. 'I'm a journalist, remember? We always protect our sources.'

He gave a great shout of laughter, unsettling the stately Spud, who began to dance a little. Then it was Casey's turn to laugh at his discomfiture, and she took full advantage of the opportunity, knowing full well he wasn't in any danger.

'Well, Miss Connolly,' he said at last, after settling the gelding, 'shall we take these two louts out for a ride?'

'Lead on, Mr Oliver,' she returned grandly. 'I'll be right behind you.'

It was the start of the most perfect afternoon on horseback Casey could ever remember. Fantasy, apparently besotted by the glorious Spud, followed behind him, as biddable as a newborn lamb, then trotted gaily at his side when they left the roads and turned off on to one of the bridleways scattered about the region. As for Jamie—Casey knew she was seeing yet another side to this highly complex man. Fully relaxed and at home in the saddle, he laughed and joked with her as though they were old friends, as though there had never been a cross word between them.

They reached an even piece of ground, and as Spud began to dance expectantly, Jamie grinned down at her. 'This fellow knows he generally gets a gallop here,' he said. 'What about you—are you up to it?'

Even though butterflies began cavorting in her stomach at the prospect, a strange exhilaration seemed to have crept into her blood. She nodded.

'I've never been able to resist challenges.'

'That's my girl.' He nodded approvingly. 'Just lean forward, come up out of the saddle a little, and let yourself flow with Fantasy's rhythm. She'll look after you. But if you feel at all unsteady, grab a handful of mane. Ready?'

She barely had time to answer before they were off and she found herself following his instructions, leaning well forward, feeling almost like a jockey as Fantasy's hoofs ate up the ground, flying like a white banner behind the still faster Spud. It was speed as she could never remmeber experiencing it before, thrilling excitement tinged with an element of undeniable fear, though she felt perfectly secure on the mare's back.

Occasionally Jamie would cast a glance back over his shoulder to check that she was all right, and she was able to grin back at him, part of her wishing this glorious chase need never end, even as another part wondered if she could survive to the finish.

At last Jamie began to slow Spud, and Casey followed his lead, sitting back in the saddle and feeling the reins. The mare obediently geared down and trotted happily alongside Spud, the two animals breathing a little more heavily after their run.

'How did you like that?'

'It was fantastic!' Buoyant still from the excitement, high on relief because she was still in the saddle and still in one piece, Casey was smiling widely as she looked up at him. 'Although I wasn't at all sure I'd be able to find the brakes once we got started!'

He nodded. 'That's why I was careful to stay in front. I knew Spud wouldn't cart me off into the wide blue yonder, and I was fairly confident Fantasy would stop when he did.'

'Fairly confident?'

He shrugged his broad shoulders philosophically. 'With horses you can only know for sure when you try. If you want a sport that comes complete with guarantees of safety, you should stick to tiddlywinks.'

She shook her head solemnly. 'Uh-huh. I had a friend who once got a tiddle stuck up her nose.' She tilted her head to one side as if trying to remember the details. 'Or was it a wink? I can't quite recall.'

She was rewarded by his laughter, a rich booming sound that rang in the trees and set the horses' ears twitching. It also started up a warm little glow deep in the recesses of her heart. She tried to quench it, but the warmth spilled over till there was nowhere more for it to go but into an answering smile that lit her eyes from within.

'You look good when you smile like that,' he said, with an abruptness that suggested the admission had been torn from him. 'You lose all tension, all reserve.'

'Am I usually so tense and reserved, then?' Letting the mare amble quietly alongside Spud, Casey shot Jamie a puzzled look.

'With me you are.' He slid her a measuring

glance. 'The only other time I've seen you fully at ease was with Lisa's pups. I felt then I was seeing the real Cassandra Connolly—not the one who appears on my television screen, so competent and sure of herself, but a warm, compassionate woman who cared more about animals than her own image.'

For a moment his words robbed her of speech. Was this really some kind of breakthrough? Was he finally coming to accept that she was more, much more, than the shallow, status-conscious individual he had originally taken her for? The possibility and all it seemed to open up before her was too great to take in, and she rode along in silence, absorbing the sights and sounds of the beautiful Cumbrian countryside, without really being aware of anything at all.

So engrossed was she in her own thoughts, she failed to see the bird which came flying suddenly out of the bushes from her left, fluttering under Fantasy's nose. The mare shied violently to the side, catching her rider completely unawares, and Casey found herself pitched into the air, coming to land on the earth with a graceless thump. Almost before she had had time to collect her senses, Jamie was at her side, kneeling down as she struggled to a sitting position.

'Are you all right?' His voice was harsh with concern.

She nodded. 'I think so. It was my own fault, I should have been paying attention.'

'Can you stand up?'

A little shakily she clambered to her feet, giving him a slightly tremulous smile. 'No harm done, other than a slightly dented pride!' She glanced over at the two horses, grazing placidly at the grass verge. 'Is Fantasy OK?'

'Perfectly. Though I think your tumble surprised her almost as much as that damn bird.' He placed his hands on Casey's shoulders and the unexpected contact sent a tremor through her. 'You gave me quite a fright too, flying through the air like that without the aid of a safety net.'

'I did?' If the fall hadn't affected her, then his closeness was certainly registering on her body, which seemed to be straining against unseen bonds to move closer to him. It was taking all the will-power she possessed not to fling herself into the strength and comfort of his arms. And yet she wasn't being honest with herself, she realised hazily—it wasn't comfort she wanted from those arms, but a lover's passionate embrace. The moment of longing was so intense it made her tremble, and nervously she licked her dry lips. 'But you said yourself that riding carries no guarantees of safety.'

Jamie smiled sardonically. 'I did, didn't I? And it still holds true—but that doesn't mean I can easily stand by and see someone. . .' he paused, his eyes searching her face as though seeing her for the very first time '. . .someone special in danger of being hurt.'

'Special?' Hypnotised by his deep blue eyes, she could only whisper the word.

He nodded slowly. 'I don't think I'd realised just how special till I saw you take that fall.' In one swift movement he pulled her into his arms, and she went with unthinking compliance, too stunned by what was happening to protest.

As she rested her cheek on the soft cotton of his shirt she could feel his heart and realised with a rush of strange joy that it was beating every bit as erratically as her own. Then his lips brushed her hair, as gently as a butterfly's wing, and she raised her head to look at him through clouded eyes.

'Oh, Casey!' With a muffled groan he cupped her face in his hands and tilted it upwards, blindly seeking her mouth with his own. His lips, tender and incredibly gentle, played over her mouth, sending sensations sweeter than molten honey coursing through her. She slid her arms about him, anchoring herself to a rock as she floundered in the sea of need he was creating. His hands restlessly pushed aside her hacking jacket, framing her slender waist, and she drew her breath in sharply, stunned by the enormity of her response to him. His touch seemed to have unleashed wild pagan forces within her, and in that moment she wanted nothing more than to fall to the ground with him, to open like a dew-wet flower to his hard naked body, and to feel the sweet warm summer air caress her skin.

'God, Casey, I want you so much!' His tortured words were muffled against her hair and she could only nod in wordless reply. For long endless moments he simply held her, his arms wrapped tight about her body. Then he gave a wry little laugh. 'But not here, my sweet. This is a well-used bridle path. I don't think we should let ourselves become an unexpected feature of someone's Saturday afternoon ride-out.'

As her pulse slowly returned to something like its normal beat, Casey became strangely embarrassed, horrified that he'd been the one to call a halt to their lovemaking. She couldn't have done it, swept away as she had been on rivers of turbulent feeling. She gave a shaky little laugh, carefully extricating herself from his embrace.

'Perhaps the fall did affect me after all,' she murmured, unable to meet his eyes. 'I can't think what came over me.'

She made to move away, but he caught her arm and she looked up at him in pained surprise.

'Hey,' he said softly, 'don't look like that. Breaking off just now was one of the toughest things I've ever had to do.' He stroked a gentle finger along her flushed cheek. 'Just a shame we hadn't been a little bit further off the beaten track.'

'It wouldn't have made any difference,' she returned stiffly. 'You simply took me by surprise, that's all. I was just about to come to my senses and push you away.'

'Really?' He raised a disbelieving eyebrow. 'And I suppose you're going to accuse me now of forcing my will on you?'

'You certainly didn't give me much opportunity to resist.' Even to her own ears the words sounded childishly petulant, and she bit her lip as he shook his head sadly.

'Casey, you do disappoint me. I'd have accused you of many things, but never cowardice.'

'Cowardice?' Her eyes blazed as she shot the word back at him.

'Yes, dammit. What else would you call it when

someone doesn't have the guts to own up to their own feelings?' There was anger in his eyes now and it was all she could do not to back away from him. 'What's wrong, Casey, hasn't anyone else ever made you feel the way I just did? Or is it just hurt pride because I had the will-power to stop and you didn't?'

'You arrogant swine! For two pins I'd——'

'You'd what, Casey?' His voice was challenging now. 'Hit me, perhaps? Go right ahead. I wouldn't retaliate. I'd never hit a woman, not even one as infuriating as you.'

'Oh, no, the great and perfect Mr James Oliver would never let himself stoop so low.' Her hands were clenched into tight fists as she squared up to him, and she grew more infuriated still to see a spark of amusement in his dark eyes. 'It would never do in this village, where they all seem to think you sit on the right hand of God, to let people know you're merely a human being after all.'

'So help me, Casey, I'd dearly love to put you over my knee and give you the walloping your parents obviously never saw fit to dish out, because lord knows you deserve it!'

At his mention of her parents all the fight suddenly went out of Casey and her face drained of colour.

'If you only but knew it, that was a very low blow,' she said quietly. 'My parents died many years ago, when I was still a child.'

He was instantly contrite. 'I'm sorry, Casey. I promise you, I didn't know.'

She shook her head. 'Forget it. It wasn't your fault.'

For a moment they were both silent, then she gave a tiny shrug. 'We'd better get back. The horses will be getting restless.'

'Are you sure you don't mind getting back on after that fall?' His voice was oddly gentle now, but in a strange way that hurt more than his insults.

'Of course not. They do say you should always get right back on after a tumble, don't they? Otherwise you might lose your nerve.' She sent him a faintly hostile look. 'And I'd hate to be accused of being a coward twice in one day.'

CHAPTER SIX

THE ride back was uneventful but completely lacking in the easy camaraderie they had shared earlier in the day. Even the horses seemed affected by the atmosphere, walking along rather listlessly, without any real spring in their step.

In the stable Casey untacked Fantasy and gave the mare a quick rub down, pleased to see she hadn't been sweating unduly, despite the rigours of the ride.

Though they hadn't said goodbye she half expected Jamie to be gone by the time she returned from walking Fantasy to the field, but to her surprise he was still there, standing beside the patient Spud. Her heart sank as she drank in the sight of him, so tall and commanding, yet so gentle as he stroked the gelding's neck and murmured quietly to him. Even after all that had passed between them she wanted him just as much as ever. And that put her in a dangerous, highly vulnerable position.

'Hi,' he said softly. 'Is Fantasy OK?'

Casey nodded. 'Having a good old roll in the muckiest part of the field she could find.'

'She deserves it—she worked well today. So did you.'

Casey smiled faintly. 'Apart from that ridiculous fall.'

'Could have happened to anyone. Even the top

riders part company with their saddles now and again.'

'Thanks.' She was uncomfortable, ill at ease, a million miles removed from the way she had felt earlier in Jamie's company.

'I'm going to ride Spud back to the kennels now.'

She nodded, miserably aware that he couldn't wait to get away. OK.'

'I'll see you later.'

She barely caught his parting words as he mounted the bay and walked off across the courtyard, but her heart was leaden as she headed back towards the farmhouse. After the afternoon's débâcle there was obviously no way he would return for dinner—why should he, when at the drop of a hat he could find himself much more amenable company? Maybe it was better this way, she told herself, without any real conviction. After all, she'd been planning to tell him as gently as possible that from now on she would manage Fantasy alone, without his assistance. This afternoon had simply saved her the trouble. So why did she feel so awful—as though a door had closed on all her fondest dreams and desires? Or as if her best friend had walked away without a backward glance?

Feeling the faint beginnings of a headache, she made a cup of coffee, kicked off her boots and threw herself down into the big old armchair in the farmhouse living-room. In a few minutes she would stir herself, find something constructive to do, instead of brooding pointlessly. But just for the moment. . .the comfort of the sagging old armchair was all she needed.

She was still there half an hour later when the noise of a car on the drive penetrated her thoughts, and she stiffened, raising her head. She certainly wasn't expecting visitors—unless it was Lisa. She never bothered with invitations.

Casey made it to the kitchen door just as the back door was opening.

'Come on in,' she called. 'I'm just putting the kettle on.'

'That's good news. I'm parched!'

The sound of Jamie Oliver's deep voice nearly made her jump out of her skin, and the shock was clear on her face as she turned towards him.

'What's wrong?' he grinned disarmingly. 'You seem surprised.'

'I thought—I mean, I didn't think—that is, I wasn't sure——' Casey abruptly closed her mouth, horrified to find herself babbling so inanely. What was it about this man that stripped her of any pretence to sophistication or poise and reduced her to an infant? she wondered hazily.

'You thought what?' He raised one eyebrow enquiringly. 'That I wouldn't be back? But you invited me to dinner.' He paused thoughtfully. 'The invitation is still on, I take it?'

'Yes, of course.' She took a deep breath, forcing herself to speak calmly. 'I simply assumed you'd be here later, that's all.'

He shrugged negligently. 'I didn't see much point in going home just to come back again, especially as I had a change of clothes in the car.' There was a faintly mocking challenge in his dark eyes. 'I thought you might not mind if I showered here.'

She swallowed hard. 'Of course I don't mind. Help yourself.'

'I will. And perhaps I could have that coffee later.'

Casey nodded, only really managing to breathe properly when he left the room, then she leaned against the Aga range, desperately in need of its sturdy support. If anyone had asked her how she felt there and then, she'd have been unable to analyse the crazy mixture of emotions. There was pleasure, she couldn't deny that even to herself, perhaps there was even a tingling of joy. But there was also confusion, dismay, fear of her own reactions—for just one glimpse of that darkly handsome face had been enough to make her knees weak. His unexpected appearance had made a nonsense of her conviction that she didn't want to see him again— now she was left wondering how on earth she could ever find the strength to tell him to go.

Belatedly realising he might not know how to work the distinctly eccentric shower, she tapped on the bathroom door, intending to call the instructions through to him. But instead of answering verbally, he opened the door, and she was instantly struck dumb. He had already stripped off his clothes—she could see them lying in an untidy heap on the floor—and was clad only in a white bathtowel slung casually about his hips.

Unable to stop herself, she let her eyes roam over him, stunned by the sheer magnificence of his near-naked body. Clothed, he was a commanding figure, but now he was like a powerful animal, his muscles rippling beneath taut skin in just the way the bay gelding's had done. But unlike the sleek, satin-smooth Spud, James's body had a liberal covering of dark hair, scattered lavishly over his arms and chest, tapering away on his flat stomach, reappearing in rich abundance on his long, muscular legs.

Her traitorous mind instantly conjured up images of how that hair-roughened body would feel pressed close to her own smooth skin, and she was weakened by a rush of desire that started deep in the pit of her stomach and spread outwards to encompass her entire being, making her giddy with the sheer headiness of it all.

Here was male beauty as she had never seen it, unblemished, unparalleled, perfection a sculptor might have carved in stone, but standing before her in warm, living, breathing glory.

'Did you want something?' His voice was oddly strained and she glanced up wonderingly.

'The shower.' She pointed vaguely in the direction of the cabinet. 'It's sometimes rather difficult. You have to know its funny little ways, or you could stand the risk of being. . .'

'Burned?' He finished the sentence for her. 'Something tells me I'm in danger of that in any case.' A slight mischievous grin lifted the corners of his lips. 'Come on then, Madam Plumber, show me how it works.'

'I could simply tell you,' she began, but he shook his head, holding out one hand to her.

'I'm not very good with inanimate objects,' he said. 'If it doesn't bark, neigh or moo, then I'm working in the dark.' He put on his most coaxing voice. 'Show me, Casey.'

She gave a tiny sigh, feeling for all the world as though she were stepping unarmed into a cage of hungry tigers.

'It's this lever here,' she explained, drawing back the shower curtain. 'You have to be careful to get it into exactly the right position, otherwise the water pressure can be terribly erratic.' She turned her head to check that he was listening, only to discover he was right behind her, his face mere inches from her own as he leaned over to inspect the lever.

'Perhaps you could just set it in the right position for me?' he suggested gravely, and his breath, fresh and minty-sweet, caressed her skin.

'Of course.' Her hands were trembling as she pressed the lever to its halfway position, then adjusted the temperature gauge. 'That should be about right,' she said shakily. 'Adjust this if you want the water hotter or cooler.' She turned to move away, but he was blocking her exit and she collided with him, closing her eyes helplessly as his uniquely male scent washed over her.

'Casey.'

At the sound of her name she looked up and knew she was lost. Her feet seemed glued to the floor as he loomed over her, his face drawing ever closer, and in the seconds before his mouth touched hers her lips parted of their own accord, their message one he couldn't fail to comprehend.

Steam from the shower dampened his skin as she pressed mindlessly against his body, aware of nothing other than the incredible sweetness of the feelings coursing through her. Nothing could ever have prepared her for this, she realised hazily—the times she had spent with Jody paled into bland insignificance by comparison.

His lips were on her throat now and she slid her hands upwards to his chest, burying her fingers in the thick pelt of damp hair, glorying in the rough sensation.

'You smell of horse,' he murmured against her hair, and she laughed huskily.

'So do you.'

'Then we'd better do something about it.' His hands swooped suddenly down over her back to clasp her backside, and she gave a muffled shriek as he lifted her clean off her feet, holding her tight against him as he stepped into the shower.

'Jamie! For goodness' sake, I'm fully dressed!' She struggled vainly against him, making no impression against his vastly superior strength.

'I thought you might appreciate my attempt to save you time by washing your clothes at the same time.' He grinned widely. 'But if not. . .'

Before she even had time to realise what he had in mind, he was tugging her sweatshirt over her head. She opened her mouth to protest, then closed it again. She couldn't stop this—it had been building between them ever since the first time she'd spotted him standing beside her own mare.

'This is crazy,' she managed to murmur, kissing his wet shoulder as he bent to pull off her socks.

'Sure is, lady.' He shot her a look of pure wickedness, drops of water glistening on his dark eyelashes. 'You want to return to sanity?'

Casey shook her head, laughing helplessly as he struggled with her jodhpurs, even more skin-tight than normal now they were soaking wet. But the laughter died in her throat as he stood again, carelessly throwing his own sodden towel out of the cabinet on to the floor.

His eyes, grown darker than ever, held hers as he reached behind her for the soap, and she gasped aloud when he used it to lather her body, his long fingers lingering for an eternity over her breasts, then sliding down over her slick skin to the base of her stomach.

'Touch me, Casey,' he commanded, and as if in a trance she stroked one hand across the flat muscular planes of his stomach and trailed her nails across his thigh, revelling in the shudder that coursed through him when she finally reached his manhood, sliding her hand along its powerful length.

As the warm water cascaded over them he bent his dark head to her breasts and she groaned deep in her throat, unable to move as his tongue flickered over one aching nipple, then moved to the other, his mouth sucking and nibbling on her heated skin.

'I can't last out much longer, Casey,' he groaned huskily. 'I seem to have been waiting so long for this.'

Unable to answer in words, she simply nodded, and he grasped her by the waist, lifting her off her feet as she slid her arms round his neck, burying her head against his shoulder.

'Put your legs round me, Casey,' he whispered urgently, and she obeyed unthinkingly, anchoring herself to his solid frame.

Slowly, slowly, he manoeuvred her until he was pressing against the burning core of her need, and she gave a tiny whimper as he slid deep inside her. For long moments they simply stood there, locked together, savouring the exquisite beauty of their bodies' union. Then as one they began to move in a primitive dance of love, answering to an age-old rhythm that could never be learned, only known deep within. Casey lost all track of time, all sense of surroundings, aware only of the man holding her, and the sensations flooding her.

Overwhelmed by the magic of it all, she wanted to tell him she loved him, but bit the words back, unsure of his response, still emotionally inhibited, though she had thrown off all notion of physical restraint. At last, when she felt she could take no more of the pressure building like sweet torture within, he gave a deep resounding groan, she heard him call her name, and in the same instant she was sent hurtling over the edge of some incredible abyss into a sky that was dark and beautiful and laden with stars.

Returning slowly to earth brought with it the realisation of all they had been doing, and she hid her face in his neck, unable for the moment to see what must inevitably be triumph in his eyes.

'Casey, look at me.' His voice was inordinately gentle. 'Don't hide from me—not now.'

She raised her head a fraction, looking up at him from under her lashes. 'I can't believe we've just done that,' she said, her voice muffled against his skin.

He grinned, and she couldn't help but be amused at the hint of very masculine pride on his face.

'Well, we have,' he answered softly. 'And further-more, we're going to do it again. That is, if my back ever recovers from this particular bit of exercise!'

'Well, of all the cheek!' She swatted him playfully with one hand. 'Anyone would think you'd been holding up a great weight!'

He chuckled and carefully set her back on the ground, reaching behind her to switch the water off. 'We're going to look like two wrinkled old prunes if we're not careful.'

'Speak for yourself.' In a strange way his playful banter had released her from her shyness and she was able to march out of the shower knowing full well his eyes were still devouring the sight of her naked body. 'I believe you originally came here for dinner, Mr Oliver?' She took a bathtowel from the heated rail and began drying herself, dodging swiftly out of his reach when he made a grab for her.

'I believe you're correct, Miss Connolly.' His dark eyes gleamed back at her as he stalked slowly after her, like a lion on the trail of its prey.

'Then you'd better come and help me cook it, because frankly you've knocked me completely off schedule.' She backed away, her eyes laughing up at him.

'I do apologise.'

'So I would hope.' She sent him a reproving glance. 'Kindly don't let it happen again.'

'Never?' His voice, low and seductive, sent a tingle right through her as he caught her easily by the waist and pulled her to him.

'Well—not till after dinner at least, Mr Oliver.'

He nodded gravely and planted a kiss on her nose. 'It's a deal, Miss Connolly.'

They were like two teenagers as they prepared the meal together in the kitchen, Casey laughing uproariously at Jamie's jokes, even though she described them as the worst she'd ever heard.

'Where on earth do you get them from, anyway?' she asked despairingly as she took her seat at the table.

'From schoolkids mostly.' With his hair still damp from the shower and that irrepressible twinkle in his eyes he looked like an overgrown schoolboy himself, she thought fondly, warmed by a rush of affection for the man.

'I keep a collection of them up my sleeve to distract kids when they're worried about their pets.' He nodded solemnly. 'It usually works.'

Casey chewed absent-mindedly on a piece of chicken, her eyes never leaving Jamie as she recalled the gentle way he had dealt with Lisa on the night Cally's pups were born.

'You must have to deal with a fair amount of heartache in your job,' she ventured softly. 'Not every story can have a happy ending.'

He shook his head. 'Not by a long chalk. It's worst when a child's involved. I can never grow accustomed to the agony in their eyes when I tell them a beloved pet isn't going to pull through.'

'Did it ever happen to you as a child?' she queried. 'Did you ever lose an animal you loved?'

'Only once.' His eyes grew pensive. 'But not through illness. I grew up on a farm, and most of our animals were working stock. My father would never allow me to grow sentimentally attached to any of them—said it was bad for me and bad for the animals.'

'But there was one?' she prompted, her meal all but forgotten as he spoke, allowing her for the first time a glimpse of his own background.

'A little spaniel.' Jamie gave a little chuckle, almost as if embarrassed by the memory. 'Cute little thing with long floppy ears and great soulful eyes. We called her Judy.'

'What happened to her?' Casey knew he was finding the story hard to relate, but something was driving her to push for more, some instinct telling her that here was the key to understanding this complex man.

He grinned, but there was no warmth in the smile. 'I guess you could say she just disappeared one morning.'

'Disappeared?' Her eyebrows shot up underneath her copper-coloured fringe. 'You mean she ran away?'

'Not exactly.' For a long moment he was silent, his gaze focused on the table. Then he sighed, apparently reaching a decision. The pain in his dark eyes was naked, and the breath caught in Casey's throat at the sight. She knew he was allowing her to see him at his most vulnerable. Part of her wanted to beg him to stop now, to keep the secrets that obviously weighed so heavily on his soul. Instead she remained silent, knowing that whatever the outcome, this opportunity might never come again.

'In a sense I suppose she was kidnapped.' He

gave a mirthless little laugh. 'Kidnapped by my mother.'

'Your mother?' Belatedly Casey realised she had never heard him mention his mother before, though he had made several casual references to his father.

He nodded. 'I might as well tell you the story from the beginning.' His lips twitched wryly. 'Just warn me if I'm sending you to sleep.' He pushed his empty plate away from him and refilled both wine glasses. Casey swallowed a growing impatience, knowing he could still shut up like a clam if pushed too hard.

'My parents were an unlikely match right from the start,' he began conversationally. 'He was a farmer, a real son of the earth, bred to the soil through generations of farming stock. She was a city girl, bright, vivacious, full of life. By rights their paths should never have crossed at all but for some capricious quirk of fate that decreed they should meet. She was an actress in a touring company—not famous, but beginning to establish a reasonable reputation. Her company came to do a week in one of the local theatres, and, though he had precious little interest in such things, Dad agreed to go along to the first night with a group of friends.' He paused, taking a long sip of wine. 'As he tells it, he took one look at the pretty little girl on stage and fell in love with her there and then. Somehow or other he managed to wangle his way backstage and met the beautiful actress. And, against all the odds, he managed to sweep her right off her feet.'

Knowing the potency of Jamie's charm, Casey felt

her heart go out to the 'pretty little city girl' who had found herself bowled over by his father.

'Anyway, she finished her tour, then came right back to Cumberland, to Dad, swearing she'd given up the stage and that he was all she wanted in life. They got married, and suddenly she found herself in a totally alien environment, where there were no bouquets, no standing ovations, no audiences—only early mornings, long hard days, and endless hours of work.' His shoulders lifted in a tiny shrug. 'I think she did her best for the first year or so, but she was never really happy. Then I was born, and it did seem for a while as though motherhood might be the answer to what was missing in her life. But it was never enough—even as a child I was aware of the arguments, the long hurt silences, the slamming doors. When I was seven, she just upped and left. Took the dog Judy, but left me.'

She could hear the pain in his tightly controlled voice, echoes of the heartbreak inflicted upon him at such a vulnerable stage of his life, and she ached for him.

'Do you ever see her now?' She had to push the words past a painful lump in her throat.

'I've never seen her since the day she left,' he answered bleakly. 'That morning she sat with me in our parlour, and tried to explain why she was going. She told me I couldn't go with her because I was my father's son, and I'd be just as torn apart in the city as she'd been in the country.' His eyes flickered over her. 'I suppose in a nutshell she proved the truth of the old saying—you can take the boy from the country but you can't take the country from the boy. Only in her case it was the city.' His eyes grew hard. 'It was a tough lesson to learn, but probably a good one. I've never forgotten it. Nothing can change a person's basic character—not even love. No one could have loved a woman more than my father loved my mother, but in the end it wasn't enough.'

Casey gazed back at him, feeling a mass of conflicting emotions. Now she understood perfectly his initial hostility towards her—and she understood what Lisa had meant in saying that perhaps Casey reminded him of someone. Everything fell neatly into place—he thought she was like his mother. But with understanding came a new sorrow. His pain and mistrust had been deeply ingrained at an early age—maybe the slate could never be wiped clean.

She stared hopelessly down at her clenched hands, then raised her eyes to him. 'I'm not your mother.'

He smiled. 'No, you're not. You do have a love for country things that she never had. But I think you're driven by the same sort of ambition that wouldn't let her be still. Though I've never spoken to her or seen her since she left, I know she went back to the stage. I've even seen her name a few times in newspaper reviews.' His long fingers played restlessly with the stem of the wine glass. 'She never did make it big, but who knows? Perhaps it's been enough for her. I hope so.'

Casey took a deep steadying breath. She might never be able to convince him he was wrong, but somehow she had to try. She owed it to herself to at least go down fighting.

'I told you my parents died when I was a child,' she said abruptly, plunging straight in without preamble. 'It was a car crash. They never knew what hit them, thank God. I was left with my big sister Megan—she was seventeen at the time and she did all she could to fill my mother's place. Up until then we'd lived in the country,' she shot him a faintly accusing glance and was rewarded with a faint smile. 'My father was born in the city, but moved out when Megan was born—said he didn't want his kids to grow up in dirty streets. After they died, Megan decided the only way we could make it was to move into town. She left school and got an office job, and we managed pretty well.' She gave a faint reminiscent smile. 'Megan took her duties very seriously—she was much stricter than our parents had been. Kept my nose well and truly to the grindstone.'

'What does Megan do now?'

'Keeps an eye on me from afar!' Casey laughed affectionately. 'I can't get it through to her that I'm supposedly a responsible adult—and even though she's married now, she still treats me like her first-born. I don't suppose she'll ever really change.'

'Does she have any children of her own?'

'No, unfortunately. Perhaps if she did she'd back off from my life a little.'

'Does she try to interfere?'

'Let's just say she's an old hand at emotional blackmail,' Casey returned ruefully. 'I don't think she really realises that's what it amounts to—but she has her own vision of what my life should be, and if I'm not doing what she'd like me to do she tends to wade in rather heavily.'

'How much does she actually influence what you do?'

Casey had to think about that one. 'To be honest, I'm not really sure,' she said at last. 'When I was younger I'd sometimes do exactly the opposite of what she told me, just for the hell of it. But she got wise to that one, so now I'm never really positive if I'm making my own decisions or whether she's been practising some sort of double bluff on me.'

'Whose decision was it that you should leave London and come here?' He leaned forward, his dark eyes interested.

'That was entirely mine.' Casey's forehead puckered in a frown. 'Meg was furious—said I was throwing away all sorts of opportunities I'd never find anywhere else.'

'She was probably right.' He slid her a measuring glance. 'Why did you do it?'

Her heart skipped a beat. She really wasn't sure she was ready to face this conversation with Jamie— but, after his frankness, she could hardly deny him the same sort of honesty.

'When I was at school,' she began tentatively, wondering just how the tale would sound to his ears, 'my best friend was a boy. His name was Jody. I was always a tomboy,' she answered his grin with the faint flicker of a smile, 'and for years we were inseparable. We went on to the same university, helped each other study, gave each other a shoulder to cry on—all the usual things. Then he went off on a year's scholarship to America, while I landed a job as trainee with the local newspaper. We stayed in touch, but didn't see each other for several years. Then he came back to Britain and got a job in television. Funnily enough, he always said he got the idea of journalism from me,' she mused. 'But he was the kind of guy who'd have made a success out of anything he'd tried. Anyway, we met up again.' She paused, weighing up her words. 'I'm not sure why, but we started going out together. I suppose we were both so happy to be back together again, we mistook those feelings for something else. He persuaded me to go down to London to be with him, and as soon as I'd found a job I did just that.' She sighed heavily. 'It was a big mistake. As friends we were terrific—as lovers. . .' she gestured vaguely with her hands '. . .we were a total wash-out.'

'You don't have to tell me any of this,' Jamie said gently, but she shook her head.

'It's OK—I don't mind talking about it. Anyway, everything finally fell apart between us. . .'

'And you headed for cover.'

She nodded. 'I suppose you could put it that way.' Actually it was a very simplistic summing up of her decision to leave the city she had never been able to call home, but it covered the basics. In truth she had been running from the lifestyle much more than from Jody, for she'd discovered very quickly that good friendship couldn't always make the transition to love. With Jody she had been uncomfortable, ill at ease. He'd never made her heart sing as crazily as Jamie Oliver could with a single smile, and they'd both known it, though admitting as much had been tough.

Although he had never said so, she knew her leaving had been as great a relief to him as it had been to her. Deep down she still hoped they would be able eventually to return to the old easygoing friendship they had once shared, for their break-up had been no one's fault, and she was still very fond of him.

'Shall we have coffee through in the lounge?'

Caught up as she had been in her own thoughts, it took a moment for his words to sink in, but, hearing the gentleness in his tone, she smiled.

'Good idea.'

When she went through, carefully balancing a tray, Jamie was already ensconced in the comfortable old sofa, and for a moment she stood uncertainly, till he patted the empty space beside him invitingly.

'Come on,' he said softly. 'No more deep and dark secrets tonight. Let's just enjoy the evening together.'

It was a pleasant, mellow time of soft music, low lights and muted conversation. Later they went to bed together and Casey felt no strain, sliding beneath the covers and into Jamie's arms as though it were the most natural thing in the world.

Their lovemaking was slow, languorous and unhurried, each taking their time to explore the other, to savour new tastes and experiences, to climb new heights together, and finally to lie in a sweet sated tangle of limbs, drifting gently off into sleep.

Casey woke first the following morning, a smile on her lips as she realised the hair on Jamie's chest was causing the unaccustomed ticklish sensation beneath her cheek. For a long time she simply lay there, barely breathing lest she wake him. Something deep within her wanted to hold on to the moment, a moment of such pure unadulterated joy she could hardly dare believe it could ever come again. And in that moment she came face to face with something she knew she'd been evading—she was in love with Jamie Oliver. Yes, he was a supremely skilful lover, but that wasn't why she had felt such ecstasy in his arms. He'd taken her beyond the bounds of reason, lifted her to paradise with his caresses, but not just through technical expertise. The way she felt about him, he could have told her nursery stories all night long and she would still have been in seventh heaven. Stunned by the enormity of the realisation, she moved her head slightly to kiss his hair-roughened skin, and he awoke, his eyes smiling a warm welcome.

'Good morning,' he said softly.

'Good morning. Did you sleep well?' Aware of her own naked body pressed close against him, Casey felt slightly self-conscious, but with one easy movement he flipped over on to his back, pulling her with him to lie along his chest.

'What do you think?' he asked. 'I seem to recall a certain young lady wouldn't let me get any sleep.'

'Well, I like that! I——'

'I rather thought you did,' he answered, and the self-satisfied look on his face made her laugh out loud.

'You didn't seem to be suffering too much yourself,' she reminded him archly.

He shrugged. 'I was putting on a good act, that's all.'

'Is that a fact?' She treated him to her best disdainful look. 'Well, in that case perhaps I'd better get up now and leave you alone to catch up on the sleep you had to sacrifice.'

'Not on your life!' As she made to move he grabbed her by the waist, pulling her more firmly against him. 'It would seem you have another, more pressing matter to attend to first.'

'Why, so I have,' she murmured, her eyes gleaming mischievously as she moved her hips seductively against him. 'Do you have any suggestions as to how I should proceed?'

'I think you're managing just fine by yourself.' His words were a strangled groan and he tangled his fingers in her hair to bring her face down to his.

'God, Casey, I don't know what you've done to me. I can't get enough of you, you witch.'

She laughed huskily, glorying in her own power, but the laughter died in her throat as his hands took command, moving freely over her heated skin, driving her into a near-frenzy of need. He grasped her by the hips, guiding her till she was able to slide down on to him, her body receiving him willingly, hungrily, her heartbeat racing faster and faster as they moved together like one creature. Release came like a shimmering cascade of stars in a black velvet sky, and she heard her own voice crying his name, a passionate crescendo as she fell against him, holding on to the only solid reality in a world gone gloriously crazy.

An eternity later she opened her eyes to see him

smiling and she grinned lazily back, aware of a sweetly pleasurable ache through her entire body.

'Feeling OK?' he queried softly.

'Couldn't be better.' She stretched her tired limbs and felt a low chuckle reverberate through his chest.

'Don't move against me like that, or I may never allow you to get out of this bed today!'

'Who says I want to?' She sent him a coquettish glance from beneath her lashes.

'Well, if it were only up to me. . .' he let the rest of the sentence hang in mid-air. 'But there's a certain mare of Arabian descent who might just be wondering what's happened to you this morning.'

'Fantasy!' Casey sat bolt upright, guilt hitting home like a sledgehammer.

'Don't panic! She'll be all right—she's in the field, remember?'

'I know, but she always gets a feed of pony nuts at about this time. I don't want to interrupt her routine.'

'Heaven forbid,' Jamie returned drily. 'Go on, then. And if you're a good girl, I might even have breakfast cooking by the time you get back.'

He proved as good as his word. And even if she didn't particularly like eggs fried sunny side up, or bacon grilled practically to a cinder, she was prepared to concede that anything would have tasted delicious that morning, especially with such a chef in charge.

'Do you normally cook like that?' she queried casually, spearing a particularly frazzled piece of bacon with her fork and splintering it into a dozen pieces.

'Like what?' He glanced downwards at his own naked chest. 'Any objections?'

She shook her head quickly. 'None at all. I was just a little afraid you might be burned by spitting fat from the frying pan.'

He gave her a look that could have melted stone. 'Lady, after the way you heated my blood last night and this morning, I don't think I'd even have noticed a little spitting fat.'

Casey swallowed hard, giddied by another rush of desire. Would she ever be able to look at this man and not want him?

'How's Fantasy?' he asked conversationally, spreading a piece of toast with enough butter to keep her going for a week.

'She's fine,' Casey replied vaguely, her mind utterly distracted as she watched his strong white teeth bite into the toast. Such beautiful lips he had—lips that could be soft and tender, beguilingly erotic in exploration, almost savage in the height of passion.

'Casey.'

'Pardon?' She blinked, taken by surprise.

'You're staring at my mouth,' he pointed out, clearly amused. 'What's wrong? Do I have crumbs on my lips?'

Unable to think of a better excuse at short notice, she nodded.

'Then why don't you just lean over here and lick them off for me?'

The invitation in his thrillingly husky voice turned

her knees to jelly. But as he leaned over the table towards her, she found herself moving closer, driven by something she no longer had any control over. It seemed to take an eternity, but when their lips finally met she closed her eyes helplessly, held completely in his thrall. His mouth moved over hers and the mingled tastes of butter and coffee on his tongue were headier than the most potent wine. She could happily have stayed there for the rest of the morning, just drinking in his kisses, but the moment was suddenly shattered by a loud buzzing noise. Bewildered, she drew back, her tawny eyes confused.

'Damn,' said Jamie succinctly. 'It's my beeper.' He reached into the pocket of his jeans and the noise ceased. 'I'm on call today,' he explained resignedly. 'That signal means I'm needed somewhere. Can I use your phone?'

'Of course.' She waved towards the hallway. 'You know where it is.'

Minutes later he returned, pulling on a shirt as he walked. 'Emergency at one of the farms,' he said briefly. 'I've got to get down there as fast as I can.' He gave her an apologetic smile. 'I'm sorry about this. Animals can't seem to learn not to fall ill at weekends.'

She shook her head. 'Don't be silly. Of course you must go.' She paused, aware that she was missing him before he'd even gone, but reluctant to put any kind of pressure on him. 'Will you be back later?' she asked hesitantly.

He grinned broadly. 'Of course. I haven't had my third slice of toast yet.'

Relief washed over her like a wave. 'Then I'll keep it warm for you.'

'You do that.' He bent to drop a kiss on her hair. 'I'll be back as soon as I can.'

CHAPTER SEVEN

'PETER, can you spare me a minute?'

Wearing the perpetually harassed look which seemed etched permanently into his features, the news editor glanced up from his typewriter.

'Yes, Casey?'

'Well, actually I need more like thirty minutes.'

'Thirty minutes?' His eyebrows shot upwards and she smiled apologetically. Asking for half an hour in a busy newsroom was tantamount to begging for gold. 'What for, Case?'

'I need a final opinion on my horse half-hour before it goes for final mixing.'

Peter's forehead creased into a frown. 'It's going out tonight, isn't it? Cutting things a bit fine if you have to make changes now.' Her gaze never faltered and he sighed. 'Aw, Case, you know I don't know one end of a horse from the other. Anyway, Micky's the executive producer. He should have final say.'

She nodded. 'I know, but he's in London attending scheduling meetings all day. He said he'd trust my judgement.'

'So?'

She gave a rueful little smile. 'I've been working on the programme so long I'm not sure I trust my judgement any more.'

Peter scratched his chin thoughtfully. 'I get your drift, kid. You're too close to it all, huh?' With a grimace he stood up. 'OK, let's go watch your masterpiece. If the newsroom falls apart in the next thirty minutes, you're to blame.'

'Thanks, Pete.'

In the small editing suite Casey stood in silence, nibbling nervously on her nails as the pictures rolled. There were many aspects of the programme to be proud of—the camera-work was good, the background research she had carried out herself flawless, and Blake had done a fine job of editing, instinctively choosing shots and camera angles which would flow together well. But still—there was one element of the piece she couldn't make up her mind about, and her tension grew as she waited for Peter's verdict.

'Terrific,' he said at last, as the closing music played over slow-motion shots of racehorses pounding the turf. 'Even to a non-horsey person like me, it's a pleasure, a fascinating glimpse into an alien world.' He gave Casey a congratulatory smile. 'Well done, kid. I especially liked that bit at the sales where you were fool enough to buy that horse.'

Casey bit her lip. He'd picked out the very section she was unhappy with.

'Are you sure, Pete?' she said uncertainly. 'Blake likes that part too, but I can't help thinking it's a bit gimmicky—as if I'd gone out of my way to get myself involved. It was meant to be more of a fly-on-the-wall documentary.'

'Nonsense! That's the bit that gives it a real human element. It even gives a non-believer like me a little insight into what makes horse-fiends tick. The look on your face when you first spotted the animal, that was terrific camera-work. It's genuine feeling—real spontaneity.'

'That's what I've been telling her all along, Pete,' Blake cut in. 'But she takes a lot of convincing.'

'Silly girl.' Pete smiled at her affectionately. 'You'll see—that's the one bit of the programme the viewers will remember and talk about afterwards. Just see if I'm not right.'

Casey felt her heart sink. She'd been counting on the news editor to see things her way, but obviously she had misjudged him. She knew she could still insist on the section being cut out—there was no shortage of material to take its place—but in the face of such opposition, she felt backed into a corner.

'OK,' she said finally. 'If you're both sure about this. . .'

'Attagirl!' Pete patted her approvingly on the shoulder. 'You'll be glad you made the right decision, I promise you.'

If only she could be so sure, she thought gloomily, making her way back to the newsroom. If pressed she would have had a hard time explaining just why she was so dead set against the piece featuring Fantasy, but somehow alarm bells had started ringing in her brain the very first time she had seen the uncut tape, and nothing since had soothed her fears, irrational though she knew they were.

That afternoon a big story broke when it was announced a local firm was to close with the loss of two hundred jobs, and working on that took her mind off everything else. On the live news programme that evening she chaired a short debate between the firm's managing director and the chief shop steward, and though she suffered a severe attack of nerves beforehand she handled the potentially explosive confrontation well, earning priase from Peter Brook.

'Come and have a drink at the pub,' he suggested. 'You deserve it after that. It wasn't an easy interview.'

She shook her head. 'Thanks, but no. I've got to get home.'

'Don't tell me you're rushing off to feed that horse of yours.' He wagged an admonishing finger. 'I know you're crazy about animals, but no four-legged friend could have put that little gleam of anticipation in those pretty eyes.'

To her amazement Casey found she was blushing. 'I do have a friend coming round for supper,' she returned loftily, unable to maintain a straight face as he crowed in delight.

'I knew it! Well, good for you, Casey—get home quickly, and enjoy your evening.'

She was still smiling as she headed her car out of the car park. Was it really so obvious she was excited about seeing Jamie? Come to think of it, why was she even bothering to ask such a rhetorical question? Every time she'd looked in the mirror over the past three weeks she'd seen the sparkle in her own eyes, the glow that Jamie had lit.

After that first evening they had spent every single night together, wrapped in each other's arms. He had been called out several times, once in the middle of the night, but knowing he would return to her warm bed afterwards Casey hadn't minded in the least. He still hadn't said he loved her and she'd had to bite the words back, fearing such an admission might drive him away. But if he hadn't spoken the words, his feelings for her were eminently clear in all he did, and little by little she was growing more confident, more secure.

Their relationship hadn't gone unnoticed in the village. Lisa had announced that she was sick with jealousy and said she'd never forgive herself for being the one who had introduced them in the first place.

'Furthermore,' she added, with irrepressible mischief in her smile, 'the entire area now has you branded as a scarlet woman. But the women sigh sadly and say "Who could blame her?" while the men nod knowingly and say "Ee, but he's a lucky lad and no mistake."'

All in all things were just about as right as they could be in her little corner of the world—if only she didn't have that tiny doubt about the half-hour special niggling relentlessly at the back of her mind.

Having seen the programme in all its various editing stages enough times to be able to recite the words off pat, she hadn't intended to watch it again on transmission, but when Jamie arrived it was clear he had other ideas.

'I've brought a couple of bottles of wine,' he announced, setting a brown paper bag on the kitchen table. 'I thought we could cuddle up in front of the TV and watch your programme.'

'I like the first part of the suggestion,' she returned with a light-heartedness that wasn't altogether genuine. 'But couldn't we watch something else?'

He raised his dark eyebrows in surprise. 'Something else? Not when I've deliberately switched night-call duty to make sure I'm not disturbed.' He ruffled her hair affectionately. 'Don't worry, Casey, I'm sure it's terrific.'

She gave a wan little smile. 'I hope you're right.'

Since they were intending to take Spud and Fantasy for a long hack the following day, Casey decided to give the mare a rest that evening.

'I think I could do with a rest too,' she admitted to Jamie as they cooked supper together in the kitchen.

'Tough week?'

She nodded. 'I don't know why, but the god of journalism never seems to spread news stories out evenly. You either get a quiet week when you're scratching round desperately looking for stories, or a week like this one has been when you have a million things to do and no time to do justice to anything.'

'That wouldn't be the case if you were still in London,' he pointed out. 'I don't imagine there would be any shortage of big news there.'

'True. But I prefer the way things are here. At least you get the opportunity to recharge your batteries every now and again.'

'Hmm.' He didn't seem convinced, and Casey's heart sank a little. He still didn't trust her—still didn't believe she wouldn't up and run at the first sight of a glittering opportunity. She found herself inwardly cursing his mother, hating the woman who had left a young boy at such an impressionable stage of his life. Her desertion had left a wound that might never really heal, she realised bitterly. But if it didn't, how could they hope to have any kin'. of future together, for surely a lasting relati nship must be based on faith in each other?

The thought stopped Casey in her tracks—up till now she had been content to live one day at a time, welcoming each new morning with Jamie as a bonus. Now she realised she wanted more—much, much more. He was the man she wanted to spend her life with, but how could she ever hope for that kind of commitment when he obviously expected her to leave as soon as the timing was right?

Subdued, she ate her supper in near-silence, absorbed in her own thoughts. Jamie tried a few times to start a conversation, but gave up in the end, obviously coming to the conclusion that nerves about her programme were keeping her silent.

When they sat down on the comfortable old sofa, he drew her into his arms and she went willingly enough, but for the first time she was aware of an inner tension, as though her body were somehow warning her to hold back before it was too late.

'Comfortable?' he murmured into her hair.

'Mmm.'

'Then relax,' he chided gently. 'Don't be so uptight. If it's less than brilliant, it doesn't matter. There'll be other opportunities, other programmes to make.'

She nodded, wishing she could dispel the growing feeling of unease. He was right, it was just another show—as Peter Brook was fond of reminding the

newsroom, an article worth even less than a newspaper feature since you couldn't even wrap fish and
chips in it afterwards.

Jamie seemed to enjoy the first part of the programme, chuckling at the sight of a toddler bouncing
along on the back of a sturdy little Shetland pony,
whistling appreciatively as the camera toured a local
racehorse trainer's stable complex. The pictures
washed over Casey in a blur. She seemed to be
concentrating so hard on his reactions, it left no
room for anything else. When he stiffened, imper-
ceptible though it was, she felt no real surprise, and
even though he made no movement she knew he'd
withdrawn from her. Realising her premonition of
disaster had come true, even though she had no idea
why, she kept her attention glued to the screen,
terrified he would see the tell-tale signs of grief in
her eyes.

'Congratulations, Casey,' he said as the last
credits rolled. She winced at the coolness of his voice.
'That was a fine piece of work. Tell me, how many
times did you have to conjure up that delightful look
of amazed joy for the camera? I had no idea you were
such a skilled actress, though God knows I should be
able to recognise the signs by now.'

'Signs? Actress?' She turned puzzled eyes towards
him. 'I don't know what you're talking about. But if
you're referring to the piece where I first spotted
Fantasy, I didn't even know the camera was on me
then. And, for what it's worth, I didn't want that
section to be included.'

'Oh, come, come,' he mocked. 'You know as well
as I do that was the real focus of the whole thing. It

was never intended just as a half-hour look at horses, was it? It was designed primarily as a showcase for Miss Cassandra Connolly—a chance to show the cool efficient newsreader has a more human side to her.' He shook his head despairingly. 'What was the plan, Casey? To sell the mare on as quickly as possible after filming? I must have been a real fly in the ointment!' He laughed mirthlessly. 'The irony being that I wanted Fantasy to be taken from you and found a home where she'd really be appreciated. But that would never have done, would it?' He held up an imaginary newspaper, pretending to scan its headline. '"TV Favourite in Horse Neglect Shock". Wouldn't have done the image much good, huh?' He regarded her steadily, his eyes hard as jet. 'This explains something else too—I always wondered why you hadn't bought a pretty little native pony, something much more suited to your limited skills. Now I understand—your beautiful Arab was considerably more photogenic. What a stroke of luck finding such an animal at the sales!' His lips curled into a sneer. 'Or had she been planted there deliberately?'

'You've got it all wrong!' Unable to take any more, she leapt to her feet, her eyes blazing. 'Of course she wasn't planted there, and I didn't buy her for the cameras. It happened exactly the way you saw it.'

'Really?' The single word dripped cynicism. 'You forget, I've had a taste of the theatrical side of life. I know how it works.'

'Jamie,' she spoke slowly, trying to contain the anger building up inside her, 'I am not your mother.'

'Perhaps not. But you share one very basic thing in common—a burning need for an audience. She couldn't live out her life away from the limelight, and, it seems, neither can you.' He paused, his lips narrowing into a thin line. 'Actually, you're probably a better actress than she was—for a little while there you almost had me believing you, believing you really did love this place, and that poor misbegotten grey mare out in the field.'

'Don't you think you're over-reacting?' She strove to sound reasonable, though her heart was rising like a trapped bird in her throat, theatening to choke her. 'All I did was visit horse sales as part of a documentary I was making in any case, and by sheer chance I bought an animal there.'

'Off your own bat, without riding her, and without a vet's examination,' he pointed out harshly. 'Doesn't that sound a little strange even to your ears, considering you could have asked any number of people round here for advice?'

'Dammit, I didn't go there intending to buy her!' Finally losing patience, she all but screamed the words at him. 'I've told you before, I simply fell in love with her.'

'Conveniently in front of the cameras.' Jamie got to his feet, running one hand through his dark hair. 'Well, don't worry—you don't have to keep up the pretence any longer. I've seen through your game.' He gave a hard bark of laughter. 'To think I should live in the country where people have real and lasting values like honesty, loyalty, integrity, and yet have the misfortune to encounter two scheming bitches who follow only the star of fame, no matter what the cost!'

'Jamie——'

'Don't bother, Casey. I'll see myself out.'

The prospect of his leaving sent panic flooding through her and her eyes were beseeching as she stared up at him. 'You can't leave like this! Surely we can at least talk?'

'Talk?' The dark blue eyes flickered contemptuously over her. 'I don't think there's anything more to say.'

As he strode from the room Casey sank back on to the sofa, its cushions still bearing the imprint of his weight. Everything had come tumbling down about her, yet it all seemed so inevitable. Things had been so perfect between them, but their relationship had been a castle built on sand—beautiful, but without foundation. Its collapse had always been merely a matter of time.

Morning found her still slumped on the sofa, gritty-eyed through lack of sleep, her throat raw from the pressure of tears she had been unable to shed. Her movements jerky and uncoordinated, she got slowly to her feet, automatically beginning to tidy the room as though in a sleep-walker's trance.

In the kitchen she made coffee, barely registering its taste as she gazed sightlessly from the window. Later she would take the pony out, and the prospect brought an ironic smile to her lips. In a world where reality had suddenly become too painful to face, Fantasy would be her only escape.

Unable to face breakfast, she immersed herself in

a long hot shower, shuddering at the unbidden memory of Jamie there with her, his bulk commanding most of the space in the tiny cabinet. As the water streamed over her skin she closed her eyes, devastated by a flood of longing as her traitorous body recalled his caresses.

It was then that the tears came, a hot flow of agony triggered by the awareness of all she had lost, and all through no fault of her own. She'd been tried and found guilty on the flimsiest of evidence, but his prejudices ran so deep she could never hope to convince him he was wrong.

She was in the middle of dressing when the telephone rang, but the faint spark of foolish hope perished when she heard Megan's voice.

'Jody's trying to get in touch with you,' her sister announced in her usual abrupt way.

'Jody?' Casey frowned, bemused. What on earth could he want?

'Why haven't you given him your phone number, for goodness' sake?' Megan demanded.

Casey gripped the receiver a little more tightly. 'There didn't seem much point,' she said carefully. 'Jody and I are finished—or had you forgotten?'

Megan gave a snort of annoyance. 'Don't be ridiculous. Just because you're no longer romantically involved it doesn't mean you can't still be friends. In any case, he's a terrific contact for you.'

'Contact?' Casey pressed two fingers against her temple, feeling the faint beginnings of a headache. 'What do you mean?'

Megan sighed with ill-concealed impatience. 'I swear, I should have been the career woman in this family and left the job of housewife to you. Don't you have any ambition in your soul, girl?' Without waiting for an answer, she pressed relentlessly on. 'Jody called me last night. He's been offered a terrific new job, co-presenting an evening current affairs programme.'

'That's wonderful!' Casey smiled, genuinely glad for her old friend. 'I always knew he had it in him. But what does this have to do with me?'

There was a second's silence, and even though Casey couldn't see her face she knew exactly the expression her sister would be wearing—one of smug triumph. 'He's been told he can help select the other presenter. The producers want a team with a special rapport. He wants you.'

'Me?' Casey's voice shot up an octave. 'Why me?'

'Because you're good at woodwork!' Megan's voice exploded along the line. 'Why do you think? Because he knows you're good at your job, and he knows you could work well together.'

'I'm not interested.' Casey spoke quickly, wincing in anticipation of a tirade. Megan didn't disappoint her.

'Not interested? Have you gone completely mad? This could be the opportunity of a lifetime—all sorts of doors could open up to you through this.'

'Meg, please, hear what I'm saying. I don't want those opportunities—I never have. I don't want the sort of life where there's no room for anything but career. I don't want to sacrifice everything I have to climb some professional ladder.'

'And what about the sacrifices I've made. Don't they count for anything?'

Casey closed her eyes wearily. It was an old familiar tune, played every time Megan wanted her to do something she didn't want to do. But even though the ploy was well-worn, it was effective. She owed her sister a huge debt for the years when she had gladly put everything in her own life into second place to ensure Casey wanted for nothing.

'Look, Meg, I know you did a lot for me. I know you gave up things, but I——'

'You don't know the half of it, miss,' Megan cut in grimly. 'What I said a moment ago wasn't entirely in jest. I should have been the career woman. I should have made something out of my life instead of constantly taking a back seat.'

'But surely you wouldn't change your life now? You're happy, aren't you?'

'Oh, I'm happy enough. But things could have been very different. If I'd taken the chance when I had it, and gone to university——' Megan stopped abruptly and Casey felt a cold hand clutch at her heart.

'University?' she echoed weakly. 'But you've always told me——'

'I've always told you I hated school and couldn't wait to leave.' Megan's voice was quieter now. 'I know I did. It was a lie. But how could I possibly have gone to university when you needed a home, a family?' She sighed heavily. 'I'm sorry, Case, I always swore I'd never tell you that. You just made me so damn mad it slipped out.'

Casey leaned her forehead against the wall, the weight of her sister's words sinking in.

'Anyway, now you know why I've always pushed

you so hard. I wanted you to succeed for both of us, for——'

'For Mum and Dad.' Casey finished the sentence for her.

'They would have been so proud to see you on national television,' Megan said softly. 'Will you at least talk to Jody?'

Casey swallowed hard on a lump forming in her throat. In less than twenty-four hours her life had been turned inside out, and Megan's revelation had shaken her to the core. She nodded weakly, knowing she was losing control of her own destiny, but unable to fight it. 'All right, I'll talk to him.'

'Good girl.'

Desperately needing to clear her mind of all its confusion, Casey rode Fantasy along the same bridleway she had followed with Jamie just a few weeks before, recklessly urging the mare into a flat-out gallop as soon as they reached the straight stretch. Today she had no awareness of fear whatsoever, just a wildness in her blood that sent caution to the four winds. It was as if she were challenging fate to do its worst, and as the world skidded past her at breakneck speed she laughed out loud, feeling alive for the first time since Jamie had walked out of her home. Fantasy seemed infected by the same exhilaration, her hoofs hardly seeming to touch the ground as she flew along, her silver mane and tail streaming in the breeze.

Trotting sedately back along the path, Casey patted the mare's neck, feeling a new strength born of defiance.

'I can't let her do it to me, girl,'she said aloud. 'I owe her a lot, but I can't let her live her life through me. When it comes right down to it, we must all make our own decisions, and this is mine. I can't do without all this.' She leaned forward to pull one of the white ears affectionately, chuckling when Fantasy tossed her head impatiently. 'Jamie Oliver can go to hell! You and I can see this thing through together—and maybe, just maybe, he'll eventually see he's been wrong about me.'

Turning into the stable-yard, Fantasy shied to one side at the unexpected sight of a horsebox.

'Well, if I wasn't sure before I am now!' A middle-aged man jumped down from the cab, a broad grin creasing his weatherbeaten cheeks. 'Our Annabel never did like this vehicle.'

'I beg your pardon?' Casey soothed the pony, feeling a faint flicker of unease.

'That's my mare you're sitting on, lass.' The man's grin never wavered.

'There must be some mistake. This is my mare. I bought her a few months ago at local horse sales.'

'Sorry, lass, there's no mistake.' There was sympathy in his nut-brown eyes. 'Annabel was stolen from us. I had no idea what had happened to her till I saw your programme last night and saw you buying her. I'd have known her anywhere.'

'Do you have any proof of this?' Casey felt as if she were floundering in a thick sea of mud.

'That I do. I can supply as many witnesses as you care to ask for, and a whole batch of photos as well.'

'That might prove you once owned her, but how

am I to know she'd been stolen?' Casey attempted to brazen it out.

'I've still got her papers.' He eyed her curiously. 'Didn't you question why a full-bred Arab was being sold without papers—a record of her breeding, that sort of thing?'

Casey shook her head miserably. 'I was so besotted with her I didn't even get a vet to examine her before buying,' she admitted.

He laughed. 'Can't say I blame you. She's a fine-looking girl. Turned a few heads in her time—and she's got a whole heap of rosettes back home.'

'If she was stolen, why didn't you have someone looking out for her at the sales?' Casey asked. 'And wasn't it a little foolhardy of the thieves to sell her at such a public place?'

'She was taken from us more than a year ago,' he said. 'I'd given up hope of ever seeing her again. Thought she'd have been taken miles out of the country by now—maybe even abroad. And you probably bought her from whoever the thieves had sold her on to. As like as not they didn't know they was handling stolen goods either.'

Casey hung her head, bowed down by sheer pain. After all that had already happened, the prospect of losing Fantasy cut like a dagger.

'How did you find me?'

The question seemed to amuse him. 'Find you, lass? Not much a problem when everyone for miles around knows where you live.'

'They do?'

'Course they do. This isn't the city where folks don't even seem to know their next-door neighbours half the time. Country ways is different. When you moved here, everyone knew within days that a television celebrity was living in the old farmhouse.' He scratched his grizzled chin thoughtfully. 'T'was well known you'd got yourself a horse too, only it somehow didn't occur to me it could be our Annabel. And you haven't been seen riding her much.'

'I stuck to the fields to begin with, just to get used to her.' Casey dismounted slowly.

'I really am sorry about this, lass,' he said gently, seeing the distress in her sherry-coloured eyes. 'You obviously think a lot of the pony—she's looking as fit as a fiddle.'

Casey nodded, unable to speak. She laid her face against Fantasy's neck, breathing in the animal smell, warm and rich. It was a scent that had never failed to intoxicate her, but now it threatened to unman her completely, and after a moment she stood back, angrily dashing one hand over her eyes.

'I suppose you want to take her right away,' she said curtly, nodding towards the horsebox.

He looked at her uncertainly. 'That was my intention,' he said slowly. 'But there's no real hurry. If you want to hang on to her for a while, I dare say——'

'No,' she returned abruptly. 'It would be as well to get it over with.' She gave him a bleak little smile. 'No point in prolonging the agony. And you've got the box here.'

He nodded, obviously uncomfortable. 'I'll need to let the police know about this. They'll no doubt come and see you, try to track the thief down.'

'Fine.'

'And perhaps we could try to work out some kind of compensation to make up for the expense you've had.'

Casey shook her head, feeling that if he said one more word it would shatter her into a million pieces. 'Please don't. I've loved having her.'

'Oh, well.' He paused, rubbing his chin. 'Doubtless you'll have insurance of some sort. You shouldn't end up out of pocket.'

She untacked the mare in silence and rubbed her down, then helped load her into the horsebox, a fresh rush of sorrow flooding through her as Fantasy went willingly enough into the trailer, her ears pricked expectantly.

'Look at that.' The man chuckled. 'She thinks she's going to a show.'

Casey walked down the ramp without a backward glance, terrified that one more glimpse of the familiar grey mare might prove her undoing. As the box slowly drove away she entered the stable, automatically picking up a fork and beginning to clear away the straw, all the while fighting an urge to fling herself down in the golden depths and howl her pain like a wounded animal.

'My God, but you're a callous bitch!'

The unexpected voice made her jump and she turned to see Jamie at the door, his eyes hard with condemnation.

'Jamie, I——'

'I just passed the horsebox on the drive. I take it that was Fantasy?' His mouth twisted as she nodded. 'You couldn't wait, could you? I had a strong suspicion you'd get rid of her as soon as you could, but I hadn't expected even you to move this fast.' He took a single step towards her. 'What did you do, Casey? Phone the nearest dealer as soon as I left? That must have been a wonderful moment for you—getting rid of two encumbrances in one fell swoop.' He gave a harsh laugh, the sound cutting into her soul. 'It's history repeating itself. My mother shook off two burdens when she walked out on my father and me.' His eyes bored into her. 'Don't you care at all, Casey? Doesn't it matter to you what happens to her? Couldn't you have waited just a little while before discarding her? I came here today to tell you I'd find a home for Fantasy,' he shook his head despairingly, 'and here you are, already getting rid of any signs that she ever existed in your life.'

'You don't understand.' Beginning to lose her hold on reality, Casey was gripped by an insane desire to laugh. Only the knowledge that she wouldn't be able to stop till hysteria cracked open the dam of tears welling up within made her hang on to the last vestiges of self-control. Her eyes glittered strangely as she gazed back at him. 'Fantasies are but fleeting things,' she said, in a high little sing-song voice. 'You told me so yourself. I managed to hold on to mine for a little while, but now they're gone, that's all.'

He shook his head. 'No, Casey. You could have held on to those dreams because they were there in the palm of your hand, but you didn't even want to try. Obviously you want more out of life than the things you had here. Well, I wish you luck in finding whatever it is you do want, Cassandra Connolly.'

His mouth twisted savagely. 'Perhaps you should seek out my mother—you two could profitably compare notes.'

He turned his back on her then and walked away. She raised one hand to stop him, but his name died unspoken on her lips as his footsteps faded away.

That evening for the first time in months Casey spoke to Jody. His voice, familiar even over the telephone wires, was strangely comforting, and almost without realising what she was doing she agreed to meet with the producers of the new show. Then she called Peter Brook and requested some of the leave due to her, starting straight away. He was a little put out at being given such short notice, but finally agreed. Three hours later, she was sitting on the night train to London.

CHAPTER EIGHT

'THE country air seems to be agreeing with you.' Jody's mouth curved into its usual boyish grin, and Casey felt the faint warmth of remembered affection. Despite all, it was good to be back in his easygoing company. When he had met her at the train station he'd flung his arms round her and for a moment she had stiffened, but then he looked into her eyes and said softly, 'Hey, kid, we're old friends, remember? That hasn't changed.' At that she was able to return his embrace, feeling at least a part of the dull weight she was carrying in her heart slide away.

Now, sitting opposite him in the restaurant, she knew no strain, and it was a good feeling.

'Thanks, Jody,' she returned. 'You're not looking so bad yourself.'

He leaned forward, frowning slightly as he studied her features. 'However, closer inspection tells me there are shadows beneath those pretty eyes,' he said slowly. 'Is something keeping you awake nights, sweetheart?'

The question made her flinch. She had forgotten how perceptive he could be. For a moment she was tempted to unburden herself to him, to tell him all her sorrows, just as she would have in the old days. But something held the words back, something that wouldn't let her share Jamie Oliver with Jody.

144

'Just the train journey,' she lied, not quite meeting his eyes. 'They always tire me.'

'Hmm.' He was clearly unconvinced, but to her relief didn't press the issue. 'So,' he continued brightly, 'do you want to hear about this wonderful job?'

She nodded. 'Sounds like you've really landed in clover this time.'

'So can you.' He reached for her hand and the touch of his smooth, slender fingers sent a pang through her—they were so different from Jamie's strong, slightly callused hands. She glanced round the restaurant, taking in its elegant, sophisticated ambience. Jody, with his immaculate clothes and streaked blond hair, was perfectly at home here— Jamie would have been a fish out of water.

'Hey, lady, are you listening to me? Here I am telling you about the golden opportunity of a lifetime, and all you can do is gaze at the wallpaper!'

Casey blinked guiltily, aware she hadn't taken in a word he'd said. 'Sorry, Jody, must be the train lag.'

He frowned, his hazel eyes narrowing. 'That's the second time you've blamed British Rail,' he said thoughtfully. 'And I don't believe a word of it. Look, is there anything you'd like to talk about? You know I can be a good listener if I try really hard.'

She smiled. 'Not a thing. Tell me about the job.'

He continued to study her for a long moment, then shrugged, his shoulders lifting the beautifully cut material of his obviously expensive suit.

'I'll start at the beginning,' he said. 'Not long

after you left London, I started presenting a daytime chat show. It wasn't networked, just on the local station, but it did pretty well, earned decent ratings.' He toyed absent-mindedly with her fingers as he spoke. 'Anyway, it was seen by the people working on a new current affairs programme——'

'Which will be networked?' Casey cut in.

His eyes gleamed. 'Not just that,' he said. 'It's for one of the new satellite channels. It'll be seen throughout Europe.'

Casey's mouth dropped open. 'Europe?' she echoed. 'Megan didn't say anything about that.'

'I didn't tell her,' he chuckled. 'I wanted to tell you that part myself, and I know Megan's inability to keep secrets of old.'

'I'm glad you didn't tell her,' Casey said darkly. 'If she'd known about this she'd have personally dragged me to London by the hair.'

He nodded understandingly. 'She always was ambitious for you—like one of those pushy mothers who try desperately to get their darling daughters on to the stage. Remember the time she telephoned your newspaper editor to complain you weren't getting enough bylines?'

Memories of Megan's tactics brought shared laughter and triggered off another round of reminiscences, till Jody finally held up one hand.

'Enough,' he begged, his eyes still twinkling with amusement. 'If we keep strolling off down Memory Lane, I'll never manage to tell you about the job.'

'OK.' Casey settled back in her chair expectantly. 'Shoot.'

'The idea is to have the show presented by new

faces,' he grinned in self-mockery, 'or, in my case, a relatively new face. And they want a partnership, a duo with real rapport, not just two separate unlinked hosts. The producers asked me to help in the search for my partner—and I thought immediately of you.'

'Why?'

He gave her a look of surprise. 'Isn't it obvious? We're friends, we think alike, we see the world from the same viewpoint.'

Casey fell silent, considering his words. Once she might have agreed, now she wasn't so sure.

'Jody,' she began hesitantly, 'I've changed. I'm not the girl you used to know.'

'Because you've been living in the country for the past year?' he scoffed at the notion. 'Don't worry, we can soon get the straw out of your ears. You're still the same Cassandra Connolly deep down.'

She shook her head. 'I'm not so sure.'

'Then let me convince you.' His expression grew uncharacteristically serious. 'The producer can't see you till the day after tomorrow, and I've taken time off to be with you. So, let me re-introduce you to all the things you've been starved of in the past year. We'll take in a show, tour an art gallery or two, do a spot of shopping.' He eyed her tweed jacket critically. 'Looks like your wardrobe could do with a bit of a face-lift.'

'What's wrong with my clothes?' she demanded, more amused than offended.

He shrugged. 'Nothing, if you're going out for a hack. But if you're going to come back and take London by storm, you'll need to look the part.

Haven't you ever heard of "power dressing", darling?'

When she shook her head he raised his eyes to heaven in a gesture of fond exasperation. 'Just leave it all to Jody. I'll transform the country mouse into a city tiger—just see if I don't!'

He proved as good as his word. Over the next day and a half, Casey's head seemed to be in a permanent spin as he did his best to show off the adopted city he so clearly loved, spreading it out before her like a magic carpet. Ignoring protests of tiredness and aching feet, he dragged her along crowded streets, into shops and huge department stores, bewildering in their vast range of goods.

'I thought you said you did a lot of walking in the country,' he teased her the following afternoon as they sat in a café drinking coffee, Casey surreptitiously kicking off her shoes beneath the table and massaging her cramped toes. 'You should be fit enough for a gentle stroll round the shops.'

'Gentle stroll?' She sent him an incredulous look. 'That was a route march! Furthermore, when I walk in the country, I wear sensible shoes, not ridiculous creations like these.' She glanced disgustedly down at the discarded leather court shoes he'd bullied her into buying.

'They're a good investment,' he returned heartlessly. 'They'll go with lots of different outfits.'

'Hmm.' Deciding discretion really was the better part of valour, she managed not to tell him what she honestly thought of the shoes, or of the other clothes he had cajoled her into paying out good cash for. One blouse had cost more than the New Zealand rug she had been intending to buy for Fantasy before the winter. The stray, uninvited thought cut her like a whiplash—there would be no need now to buy anything for the pony, and the realisation made her eyes sting.

'Hey, don't look like that!' Jody remonstrated gently. 'I know you've spent a lot, but you don't have anything to worry about. You'll get a great clothing allowance when you start work.'

Casey summoned up a weak smile. She'd been trying desperately to concentrate her mind on the new job, and to blank out thoughts of Cumbria, but the pain was constantly there, her defences powerless against the debilitating memories of Fantasy—and Jamie Oliver. For the millionth time since stepping foot in the city, she felt a pang of agonising loss for all the things she would be leaving behind if she did return to London. But then, she reminded herself brutally, Fantasy and Jamie were already lost to her, and how empty Cumbria would be without them.

Forgetting them would be impossible, she had to accept that rationally as well as emotionally. But perhaps here in the crowded streets of the capital she might eventually be able to come to terms with her grief—back in the lush green countryside she would be reminded at every turn of rides out with Jamie and the beautiful grey Arab mare. Even the farm was imbued with their presence. For the sake of her sanity, perhaps escape to London really was the only option.

'I might not get the job,' she pointed out, striving for a lightness she was far from feeling.

Jody snorted dismissively. 'Nonsense! It's a piece of cake.'

'How can you be so sure?'

'They've already seen videos of you, and they like your style. And they agree with me that you and I will complement each other well.'

'Videos?' She ignored the last part of his statement. 'How?'

'Not difficult when you work in the TV network, Casey darling,' he returned smugly. 'I just made a couple of phone calls, that's all.'

'Without telling me?' She felt a stab of annoyance at his high-handedness. 'Really, Jody, sometimes you are the giddy limit!'

He shrugged unconcernedly. 'Seemed good sense to me. There would have been little point in dragging you down here if you'd been completely wrong for the job.'

She sighed heavily. 'I'm still not sure I'm not. Completely wrong, I mean.'

'Nonsense!' He fixed her with a stern glance. 'You lack self-confidence, my girl, but trust your Uncle Jody. I know you can do it blindfolded.'

She shook her head. 'You don't understand. I reckon I could cope with the actual work—but would I be happy?'

'Happy?' The question clearly perplexed him. 'You'd be challenged, stimulated, doubtless put to the test many times over, and I'm quite sure you'd pass those tests. And you'd be on your way to the top—just think, Case, not just national, but Europe-wide exposure. More money than you probably ever dreamed of earning, plus status and prestige.' He eyed her wonderingly. 'What's happy?'

She gazed back at him, taking in the warm hazel eyes, the endearingly boyish features, the stylish suit, and her heart sank. He'd said they shared the same view of the world, but for the first time she wondered if that had ever been true.

'Happy is when you get up on a fine summer's morning and breathe in clean fresh air,' she said softly. 'It's when you walk to the field and see a pony enjoying a good roll in lush green grass. It's when you see half a dozen brand new puppies wriggling round their mother.' She could have added that it was when the man you loved held you in his arms, but just saying the words would have devastated her.

He shook his head in obvious disbelief. 'It's just as well I came looking for you when I did,' he said. 'A few months more and you'd have been a lost cause. All that stuff's fine for those that were born to it, Case, or even for people who want to retire to some rustic idyll. But it's not for the likes of you and me—we were made to hustle—we need challenge, risk, something to send the adrenalin flowing.' His eyes raked over her face, as if searching for clues. 'Look, I know you think you love the place—frankly, you've been so distracted ever since you got here, I've had the distinct impression you've been here in body alone, and that your spirit's really back there in hillbilly heaven.'

'Don't you dare call it that!' she shot back at him, incensed by his disparaging tone. 'That's just the kind of big-city attitude I detest most.'

'That's better.' His grin was triumphant. 'That's

more like the Casey Connolly I know—I was beginning to fear the mellow, laid-back life had killed your fire.'

'My fire?' The description surprised her.

Jody nodded. 'Sure. You were always ready to do battle for things you cared about, even if you were in the wrong. Don't you remember the time you gave Susie Craig a black eye because she'd been teasing a puppy?'

'She wasn't teasing it, she was tormenting the poor little thing.' Casey grew hot under the collar just remembering the incident. 'She deserved more than a black eye.'

'She'd have got it too, if I hadn't pulled you away.' Jody's hazel eyes grew thoughtful. 'Funny, really, I'd never imagined you as a fighter, not in the physical sense, at least.'

'I'm not. But I wasn't prepared to stand by and see that little animal being hurt.'

Jody glanced at his wristwatch, then gulped down the last of his coffee. 'Come on, time's a-wasting. I want to take you to a little boutique I know this afternoon. Very exclusive.'

'And very expensive, no doubt,' she returned drily, and he chuckled.

'You have to speculate to accumulate,' he said. 'And in this case that means paying out to get something that will knock 'em flat at the interview. Now put your shoes on—I've got a feeling this little shop will have just what we're looking for.'

'Are you sure I look all right?'

Jody rolled his eyes heavenwards. 'I've told you

six times already—yes, Casey, you look terrific. Cool, calm, composed, with just a hint of underlying sensuality. They're going to love you.'

She glanced towards the mirrors covering one side of the TV station's reception area. The woman looking back was a complete stranger, a stranger who wore her copper-coloured curls in a sleek bob, who stood tall in high-heeled shoes, and who obviously bought her clothes from top-name designers, if her wool and silk mix skirt and jacket in the new season's colours of burgundy and russet were anything to go by.

'But that isn't me,' she said softly. 'That woman's an impostor.'

Jody moved to stand behind her, placing his hands on her shoulders. 'This is a glimpse into the future, Case,' he murmured into her hair. 'This is the woman you'll become—elegant, beautiful, sophisticated.'

As she stared at the mirror, the image in the tilted glass seemed to blur, and for a second Casey saw herself standing there, slender and boyish in jodhpurs and sweatshirt, her hair curling riotously about her elfin features. Instead of Jody's effortlessly stylish figure behind her, she saw Jamie, his shirtsleeves rolled back over strong, sinewy arms, his eyes lit up with laughter.

The vision was so vivid, so real, she unthinkingly reached out one hand towards him. But reality returned as her fingers touched cold, hard glass instead of warm, living skin, and pain ripped through her like a jagged knife.

'Ready?' Jody spoke softly at her side.

She nodded, unable to meet his eyes. 'As I'll ever be.'

He led her upstairs through a bewildering array of corridors to a large plush office, its décor muted and stylish. A tall, silver-haired man came forward to shake her hand.

'Miss Connolly, I'm delighted to meet you at last,' he said warmly. 'Or may I dispense with formality and simply call you Cassandra?'

'It's usually Casey,' she began, but he shook his head.

'Cassandra from now on, I think. It will look wonderful on the credits.' He patted Jody on the shoulder. 'Just as this young man must grow accustomed to being called Jonathan. Names are very important to the image, you know.'

So it was starting already, Casey thought hazily, watching Jody grimace in comic distaste. Even before she'd been offered the job, they were trying to change her—just a small change, perhaps, but a significant one. It probably wouldn't bother Jody at all—he'd happily change his name by deed poll to Nebuchadnezzar if told it would help the ratings, but Casey couldn't help feeling rankled by the presumptuousness of the man who was now showing her to a chair. He introduced himself as Sheldon Walker, head of programmes on the new satellite station, clearly assuming Casey must have heard of him. She smiled politely, deciding not to disillusion him.

'Tell me about yourself, Cassandra.' He seated himself at the other side of a large, imposing desk.

'Jonathan tells me you've been working in Cumbria—a good little station, that one, I know it well.'

'Casey felt it would be a good career move to learn the TV ropes in a small place first,' Jody cut in before she could answer, and she sent him a sidelong glower.

'Quite right.' Sheldon beamed at her. 'I did the same myself, back in the dim and distant past. But now you're ready to move on, is that it, Cassandra?'

She opened her mouth to reply, then caught Jody's warning look. 'London is generally regarded as the place to be for those with ambitions,' she said, despising her own answer. Sheldon Walker nodded approvingly.

'Quite right. Now, Cassandra, I'd like you and Jody to do a screen test together for me. Is that OK with you?'

For a moment she could only stare at him— seconds before he'd asked her to tell him about herself, yet hadn't given her time to utter more than a single sentence. She knew she was being unfair— he was a busy man, with no time for trivia—yet she couldn't help remembering her interview with Peter Brook. After the initial interrogation about qualifications and past jobs, that had settled into a pleasant little chat. He'd wanted to know Casey as a person, not just as a journalist.

'Cassandra?' Sheldon Walker's voice held a touch of impatience.

'I'm sorry. Yes, of course—a screen test would be fine.'

'Good. Then come along, both of you, I'll take you to Make-up.'

The next half-hour passed by her in something of a blur, though afterwards she could remember every second with perfect clarity. The studio was similar to the one she was accustomed to, a surprisingly small room which she knew would look very much larger on screen. One area was dominated by a marble-grey serpentine-shaped desk, another pointed out by Jody as 'the interview area' contained three soft armchairs and a low coffee-table.

The floor manager, a bulky, bearded man with an air of permanent boredom, took her to a seat behind the grey desk. Jody sent her a conspiratorial wink from his place several feet away, and shoved several sheets of paper along to her.

'They want to hear your newsreading first,' he said. 'I've already looked through your scripts—don't worry, no unpronounceable Arabic names to trip you up.'

'The scripts are on auto-cue, naturally.' The floor manager sent Jody an irritated look. 'These are purely for back-up.'

Given the signal, Casey delivered the bulletin in her usual flawless style, feeling not the faintest flicker of nerves as her eyes followed the words on the camera screen before her.

As she finished, a tall, glamorous woman with short jet-black hair and large earrings was shown to the interview area, where Casey and Jody joined her.

'This is your two-handed interview,' the floor manager explained laconically. 'Details on that sheet of paper.'

On the cue Casey faced the camera and gave an

ad-lib introduction, explaining the interviewee's identity and situation. Though she and Jody had never worked together as a team, things went relatively smoothly, and she was able to ask questions, pick up from Jody's points and watch for cues, without any real problems.

'Sheldon wants you to do another interview.' The floor manager approached the desk as Martha Hughes left the studio. 'But this time single-handed, and taking instructions by earpiece instead of relying on me.' He favoured her with a faint smile. 'Think you can cope with that?'

Since she'd used an earpiece ever since her first time on screen, the proposition held no terrors. She returned his smile with a quick nod, and the soundman reappeared to fit her up.

'That's the best I can do, love,' he said after trying several pieces. 'You've got remarkably dainty ears. You'll need to get a piece specially moulded to fit.'

'It's fine.' Casey scanned the page of information just handed to her, learning that the next interviewee was playing the part of a prominent MP, leading a campaign against having nuclear waste dumped in his rural constituency.

'Ready, Cassandra?' She heard the director's voice in her ear and gave a thumbs-up sign to camera. 'OK, it's a three-minute chat. We've got a few graphics to slot in where appropriate, so keep half an eye on the monitor and try to mention them. You'll be counted out of the chat. Try not to let it run over time.'

The interviewee this time was a short, bulky man in an ill-fitting suit, obviously determined to play his part to the hilt, with a ready supply of politician's jargon and clichés up his sleeve. Casey led the chat skilfully, never allowing him to escape with glib phrases, gently but firmly insisting he answer the question rather than wander off on his own preferred tangent.

All the while she was hearing a non-stop stream of chat in her ear as the director gave instructions to his production assistant, to the floor manager, to the sound department, and to the vision mixer. Once he even told a ribald joke that brought gales of laughter from the gallery. None of it fazed her. At the end she brought the interview neatly to a close, politely squashing the fake MP's bid to carry on talking. A telling glance between the floor manager and the senior cameraman told her she'd done well, though neither said as much to her. Jody wasn't as reticent, however. As she removed her earpiece he flung his arms round her and planted a smacking kiss on her cheek.

'That was ace, kid!' he crowed triumphantly. 'You handled all of it like a seasoned trouper—and they were throwing everything in the book at you.'

'I noticed,' she returned drily, only now allowing herself to smile at the director's joke.

'Come on, the boss wants to see us again.'

Upstairs in his office, Sheldon handed Casey a glass of wine.

'Congratulations,' he said warmly. 'That was a fine screen test. You handled things very well on your own, and, as Jonathan and I had already suspected, you made an excellent double act. I can hardly believe you've never worked together before.'

'We go back a long way,' Casey murmured.

'Well, the rapport between you is obvious.' Sheldon perched himself on the edge of the desk, waving her towards a seat. 'Now, Cassandra, obviously I can't tell you anything definite at this stage. We do have one or two other people to see,' his eyes twinkled mischievously, 'though to be honest I can't imagine we'll find a better partner for Jonathan. Unofficially and completely off the record, I suggest you return to Cumbria and begin packing.'

Casey looked down at the floor, unable to meet his eyes. She should have been ecstatic, instead all she could feel was a slight niggle of irritation—this man clearly thought he was handing her the moon on a plate, that she would immediately leap at any offer made to her, that she could shake the dust of Cumbria from her feet without a second thought. But then, she reminded herself angrily, he was entitled to think that way. People didn't generally attend interviews unless they seriously wanted the job on offer—and it was the most exciting opportunity ever likely to come her way.

She felt a rush of sadness—Cumbria and all it held was slipping away from her, and with the combined forces of Megan, Jody and Sheldon working against her she seemed powerless to stop it.

She looked up, mustering the brightest smile she was capable of. 'Thank you very much. I appreciate your faith in me.'

The two men began talking then about transmission dates and schedules, but most of the conversation went right over Casey's head and she was glad when she was finally able to escape, Sheldon's last words ringing in her ears.

'I'll call you in a couple of days,' he said. 'And if I'm any judge of anything, it'll be with good news.' Her hand was engulfed in his considerably larger paw and squeezed warmly. 'I look forward to working with you, Cassandra.'

'It's in the bag!' Jody crowed as they left the building. 'You've got old man Sheldon hooked, and he's the one with the real power in this place.' He grabbed her arm and whirled her about to face the imposing building. 'Look at it, Casey, and make it a good long look. That's where your future lies.'

'You really think so?' Try as she might to find a matching excitement within herself, Casey was aware only of an empty space.

'I know so.' He cocked his head boyishly. 'Until the next bigger, brighter and even better job offer comes along that is. Come on, Case, let's go celebrate.'

She gave him an apologetic little smile. 'I'd rather not. It's too much like counting chickens before they're hatched. What I'd really like to do is spend a couple of hours wandering round by myself. Do you mind?'

He gave her a slightly suspicious look, then nodded. 'I get it. You just want time to take it all in, huh? OK, honey. I'll come by your hotel later and pick you up. We can make a celebratory night of it.'

Gripped by a sudden desperate need to be alone, she nodded, ready to agree to anything.

'Seven-thirty? Wear something pretty.' Then he

kissed her on the cheek and was gone, moving with the quicksilver speed that had always characterised him. Casey smiled softly—ever since she'd first known him, Jody had been in a rush, always hurrying to get somewhere else. Excited as he was about the new job, she knew perfectly well his sights were already on the next challenge, the next rung on the ladder.

Casey started walking along the road, mentally cursing the high-heeled shoes that made strolling a chore rather than a pleasure. The television studios were situated in a particularly busy part of London, and within minutes she was tired—tired of pushing past people on the pavements, tired of the nameless faces, none of them wearing a smile or calling out a cheery greeting, tired of the never-ending line of traffic streaming past her.

Disregarding her aching feet, she trudged on, barely noticing the endless array of shops with their brightly coloured displays and tempting offers. Finally she spotted a sign for a park and headed gratefully towards it, feeling she'd die if she didn't see a patch of green soon. In truth, it wasn't much more than a patch, just an overgrown garden with a scattering of benches, but she sank thankfully down on to one of the hard wooden seats, feeling she'd reached some sort of sanctuary.

If she took the job, there'd be precious little opportunity for relaxing on park benches—little time to simply sit and smell the flowers and let the rest of mankind go by. She would be entering a new world—a world of stress and high tension where she would constantly have to be looking forward for new opportunities, but at the same time watching out for all the hungry young pretenders just waiting for the opportunity to prove they could fill her shoes more ably than she could. It was a world she knew—she had watched it from the sidelines when she'd lived in London before, and she'd been more than happy to leave it behind when she went to Cumbria.

Did she really want to become a part of all that? She frowned, unthinkingly scuffing one expensive leather court shoe on the gravel beneath the park bench. In truth the job held no appeal whatsoever—she'd told Jody she could handle the work, and she had meant it. Although she had proved lamentably weak in some areas of her life, she'd never had any qualms about her professional capabilities. But she enjoyed working on the small Cumbrian station, enjoyed the variety it offered, enjoyed the camaraderie of the staff. If it was a straightforward matter of swapping one job for the other simply for the job's sake, she would have no hesitation in turning the London option down. But it wasn't as simple as that.

Casey's sherry-brown eyes grew wistful as she stared unseeingly at a much trodden-on piece of grass. If she took the London job, it would be for one reason and one reason only—to get away from all the memories of Jamie and Fantasy. Not that the trip south had done anything to ease her pain so far, she acknowledged ruefully—even when she'd been concentrating on the studio interviews, Jamie's dark, laughing eyes had never been out of her mind. The distance she had put between them had only increased her longing for him, but surely—please

God—the sheer agony of that longing must eventually diminish if only she didn't have to cope with the ever-present danger of bumping into him? Not that she believed in the old saying of 'out of sight, out of mind'—where he was concerned, that was little more than a foolish dream—but she could never hope to let the wounds heal over if she kept seeing him, kept experiencing that crazy spurt of hope only to have it savaged by the look of contempt she knew only too well.

She was caught between the devil and the deep blue sea, she realised—damned if she did go to London, to a life she knew could never make her happy, even more damned if she stayed in the home she loved so very much, but which held such treacherous pitfalls. Moving south would mean ruthlessly, brutally stamping on all her own emotional needs—staying in the north would destroy her by degrees.

She lost track of time as she sat there, immersed in thought, but eventually as the air began to grow cooler she got to her feet with a heavy sigh. It was time to go back to Cumbria, time to start pulling up roots, time to start making farewells. Jody's evening of celebration would have to wait.

CHAPTER NINE

CASEY arrived home late that night, weary and low in spirit. Feeling grimy after the journey, she took a long hot shower before collapsing into bed, exhausted body and soul. The radio alarm at her bedside clicked on at its usual time the following morning, but she slept right through the disc jockey's genial chatter, the news bulletins, weather reports and music. Yet when she awoke she was still far from refreshed, aware of a fatigue that seemed set deep into her bones.

Automatically she moved about the house, fixing breakfast she couldn't face eating, unpacking her case and hanging up her new purchases with a feeling of revulsion for the elegant clothes, then skimming briefly through the mail that had accumulated in her absence. None of it was important, so she left the envelopes on the kitchen dresser to be dealt with later.

Feeling a need for some fresh air, she dressed in jeans and a sweater, picking up a lightweight jacket in case the day should prove cooler than the beautiful blue skies promised. It had been a terrific summer, but autumn was on the horizon now and the Cumbrian weather was notoriously fickle.

Outside she stopped for a moment to let the clean cool breeze wash over her, drinking in the country silence that really wasn't silent at all, with its sounds of birdsong, the rumble of a far-off tractor, and a dog barking somewhere in the distance all combining to create a melody she knew she would never tire of hearing.

Aimlessly she wandered across the courtyard, leaning on the gate and propping her chin on her hands as she gazed into the field. It was empty now, but one muddy patch still bore the marks of hoofprints and the sight sliced into her, cutting through the fog which seemed to have been clouding her brain ever since she had got up that morning. She would never have believed it was possible to be so devastated by the loss of an animal—but now she dropped her face into her hands, swamped anew by the pain. Fantasy had been more than a pony, she realised bleakly—she had represented the fulfilment of all the childhood dreams that had been so cruelly torn away from her with the death of her parents. Losing the pony had been like losing a part of herself.

Now the tears came—tears she hadn't been able to shed when the horsebox carried Fantasy away, tears she had denied herself when Jamie had accused her of callously discarding the pony to suit her own selfish ends. It was as though a dam had broken within her, a dam which had been holding back all the pent-up sorrow behind a wall of stone.

'Hey, hey, what's this?' Suddenly two strong hands grasped her shoulders and turned her round none too gently. Taken entirely by surprise, she raised her eyes to see Jamie, and the shock triggered another onslaught of sobs.

'What's wrong?' His voice was urgent. 'Why are you crying?'

'What the hell does it have to do with you?' Dismay at being found like this, by Jamie Oliver of all people, made her belligerent. 'No doubt you'll make up your own mind anyway, just as you always do.' Her voice cracked on a sob as she searched her pockets for a tissue. 'Look behind the tree, why don't you? You'll probably find a television camera skulking there to get shots of me crying—just to show the "other side of Casey Connolly."' Giving up on finding a tissue, she wiped one hand angrily over her eyes.

'Here.' He thrust a large white handkerchief at her. 'Come on, Casey. Something terrible must have happened to make you cry like this.'

'Something terrible?' She glared up at him, feeling a crazy desire to laugh. Could he really be so unaware of all she'd been going through? 'Why should I tell you anything, when you won't believe it in any case?'

'Try me,' he said gently.

Unable to meet the sympathy in his dark eyes, she hung her head. 'I'm crying for Fantasy,' she said, the very act of saying the pony's name enough to send a fresh flow of tears to her eyes.

'For Fantasy?' His hands tightened on her shoulders as he frowned uncomprehendingly. 'But you sold her.'

'No, I damn well didn't!' Incensed, she shook off his hands and took a step back, unconsciously squaring up to him. 'You simply assumed I did, because it fitted in with what you wanted to believe about me. But the truth of the matter is, she was taken from me, by her real owner.' Casey shook her head, trying to rid her mind of the image of the silvery grey pony walking so gaily into the horsebox. 'She'd been stolen, you see,' she went on softly. 'I didn't know that, of course, but her owner saw her on that documentary I did on horses.' She gave a little mirthless laugh. 'Ironic really, isn't it? You thought that had all been a set-up to make me look good in front of the cameras, yet if you but knew it, I'd all but begged the film editor not to use the shots of me buying her. I must have had some sort of premonition.'

'Stop, Casey, back up a bit.' Jamie's eyes searched her tear-stained face. 'Are you telling me the man in that horsebox was Fantasy's real owner?'

She nodded miserably, and he swore softly under his breath.

'Why in God's name didn't you tell me that at the time? Why did you let me believe you'd sold her?'

'Let you believe?' She sent him an incredulous look. 'Are you kidding? You never gave me a chance to explain. Frankly, I don't think you'd have believed me even if I had.'

'Hell's bells, what a mess!' He raked his fingers through his dark hair. 'I take it he did have proof of ownership?'

Her eyes narrowed. 'What now, Jamie? Are you belatedly trying to take charge of the situation? Yes, he had proof—he had the papers for Fantasy, or rather Annabel, since that's her real name. If you remember, you asked me about her papers the first night we met.'

'You said they'd been lost.'

'Obviously someone along the line was telling lies.'

He nodded. 'Can't really blame you for believing it, though—these papers are forever going missing.' He eyed her thoughtfully. 'Haven't you considered getting another horse?'

She shook her head. 'At first I couldn't face the thought of replacing Fantasy—she was just so special to me. And now. . .' she turned her head to gaze out over the field as if imprinting it on her memory. '. . .now there's no point.'

'No point? Why?'

'Because I'm leaving.' It was an effort to say the words, and she gasped aloud as he suddenly gripped her arm, his fingers digging into her tender flesh.

'What did you say?' he demanded harshly.

'You heard.' She lifted her chin defiantly. 'I'm leaving Cumbria and going back to London. So you see, you must have been right about me all along. Don't you feel positively vindicated?'

'Let's leave me out of this for a moment,' he said through gritted teeth. 'Why are you leaving?'

'I've been offered a superb job with one of the new satellite stations as co-presenter of a news and current affairs programme. Just think,' she taunted, 'I'll be famous all over Europe. Pretty good, huh? Better than your mother ever achieved.'

His eyes darkened and for a second she thought he was about to strike her. 'I'll forget you said that,' he ground out. 'So this is really what you want, is it, Casey?'

She opened her mouth to answer him in the

affirmative, but the look in his eyes defeated her, and she was forced to blink away a fresh rush of tears. 'No,' she whispered. 'No, damn you, it's not what I want.'

'Then why are you taking the job?'

'Because I can't see any other choice. There's nothing left for me here.'

'I thought you loved the place.'

'I do!' Anguish was written clearly on her features. 'Cumbria has become my home—I haven't felt that way about anywhere else since my parents died. I love everything about it—its beauty, its wildness, its freedom. I love the fact that I can walk along the middle of a country road and have very little fear of being knocked down. I like saying hello to people and getting a reply, even if they're total strangers.' She paused, a sad little smile playing about her lips. 'But at least in London there won't be anything to trigger the memories I can't cope with here.'

'And what do you intend to do with those memories?' he queried quietly. 'Bury them away in your heart?'

She nodded.

'You'll be living only half a life, Casey.'

'Better that than the hell I'm living now.'

There was silence between them for a moment, then he relinquished his hold on her arm, only to slide his hand downwards to close over her nerveless fingers. 'I came up here today because Lisa told me she hadn't seen you for several days. She was concerned.'

She waited, wondering what point he was trying to make.

He smiled. 'You have friends here, Casey. People who care for you.'

'People like you, you mean?' She couldn't keep the bitterness from her voice. 'People who'll offer friendship, then snatch it away because of something they *think* I've done?' She shook her head. 'Friends like that I can do without, thank you very much!'

'Is that all we were, Casey?' He spoke the words so quietly she barely heard him. 'Friends?'

She tried to glare at him, but the warm pressure of his hand on hers made her heart move within her. 'What else?' Her attempt at a sneering answer didn't quite come off.

'I think we were a lot more than that,' he said. 'And I think that's why things went so badly wrong. If we'd been just friends, I'd probably have contented myself with giving you a bawling out for selling Fantasy, but I'd certainly have stuck around long enough to hear the truth—and I'd probably be standing here right now congratulating you on your new job.'

'I don't want your congratulations,' she said moodily.

'And you're not going to get them.' His eyes regarded her steadily. 'If you go to London, it'll be the biggest mistake you ever made.'

She gazed up at him in astonishment. 'You've changed your tune, haven't you?' she said. 'I thought you were convinced all the way along the line that the be-all and end-all of my life was ambition.'

Jamie lifted his free hand to stroke her cheek, and she steeled herself not to dissolve at his touch.

'You once accused me of being incapable of changing my mind even when I was wrong,' he said. 'Now I think you owe me an apology, because I have changed my mind—about you.'

'Why?' She breathed the word, barely able to believe the warmth in his dark-sea eyes.

'The power of a woman's tears,' he said softly. 'I don't believe I've ever seen anyone as desolate as you were when I first arrived. No one could fake that kind of agony—and you weren't even aware you had an audience.' He paused. 'Were those tears solely for Fantasy?'

Casey felt her face grow warm under his searching gaze. 'No,' she mumbled. 'I think I was crying for all the things I'm about to lose.'

'Then don't lose them.' His answer was immediate. 'Have you accepted the job offer?'

'No, but——'

'Then turn it down.'

'But I——'

'Look, Casey. I want to apologise to you. I've treated you shamefully, but I want to make it up to you if that's at all possible. And if I can do my bit to stop you from making what could be a colossal mistake, then I'll consider myself satisfied.' He lifted a stray tendril of auburn hair from her cheek and tucked it behind her ear. 'I've seen you drink in the sweet country air, Casey Connolly—I've seen your eyes fill with delight at the sight of a rippling river, or a new-born pup. I think you'd suffocate in

London's busy streets. And I think you know that too.'

'Why should it matter to you what I do?' she breathed, feeling as though his tender words had swept the ground from under her unsteady feet.

'Because I care for you—and that's been the problem all along. If I hadn't cared for you, I'd never have gone off like an Exocet missile.' He smiled self-mockingly. 'That's always been a bad habit of mine—just ask Lisa. She's been on the receiving end of a few blistering attacks in her time.'

His words hit Casey like a blow in the stomach. He 'cared' for her—but only in the same way as he cared for Lisa. He'd finally realised he'd been wrong about her—but the feelings he admitted to fell horribly short of the way she felt about him. Valiantly she struggled to swallow hard on the lump forming in her throat—she should be pleased, shouldn't she? At least she didn't have to deal with the agony of believing he hated her any more.

'Will you at least think about what I've said?'

For a long moment she simply stared at him, then she dipped her head. 'Yes, I will.'

'Good girl!'

Two days later Casey awoke with a start, the sound of loud banging shattering her dreams. For a moment she was completely disorientated, glancing down at her own fully clothed body, then at the television chattering quietly to itself in the corner of the room, then she realised that once again she'd slept the whole night through on the sofa. A crick in her neck and a faint ache in her back told her it hadn't been a terrific idea, and she groaned as she levered herself to her feet.

'OK, OK, I'm coming!' More than a little bit out of sorts, she made her way to the back door, scowling as sunlight hit her eyes.

'My, but we are a grouch this morning! Is the kettle boiling? I'd have let myself in, but the door was locked.'

'Morning, Lisa.' Casey flapped an ineffectual hand in the other woman's direction, vainly attempting to cut off her flow of chat.

'Not suffering from a hangover, are you?' Lisa's pale blue eyes narrowed as she surveyed Casey's white face and shadowed eyes. 'You look just like Joe does when he's been celebrating too vigorously!'

'Thanks.' Casey sent her the ghost of a smile. 'Actually, I haven't touched a drop.'

'Well, you look awful,' Lisa said frankly. 'Desperately in need of some good healthy fresh air.' She switched the kettle on, then frowned. 'Where's the sugar this time? Beside the shoe polishing kit, maybe?'

'I doubt that, since I don't possess one.' Casey couldn't help but chuckle at the sight of Lisa on her hands and knees, searching the bottom cupboards for the elusive sugar.

'Got it!' With a satisfied grin, she sat down.

'So tell me,' Casey eyed her curiously, 'what brings you here at such an unearthly hour on a Saturday morning?'

'Unabashed nosiness,' Lisa returned blithely. 'I want to know what you were up to yesterday.'

Casey frowned. 'Yesterday? Why?'

'Because I happen to know you were looking at farmhouses, which I also happen to know are for sale.'

Casey's mouth dropped open, then she began to laugh. 'Why I should be in the least bit surprised at your knowing that, I really don't know,' she said. 'I've always said the jungle drums in this part of the world work much more efficiently than any official news service.'

'Well, of course,' Lisa agreed complacently. 'This is the country. So come on—fill in the gaps for me. What's the real story?'

Casey sat down at the kitchen table with a sigh and reached for her coffee-cup. 'I was in London earlier this week,' she said, sending Lisa a wary glance. 'Did you know about that too?'

The other woman had the grace to look a trifle shamefaced. 'Actually I did. Jamie told me.'

Casey rolled her eyes heavenwards in mock exasperation. 'And you know why I was there?'

Lisa smiled assent. 'So—if you've been looking for a place to buy, does that mean you've decided to turn down the job?'

Casey nodded.

'Well, hallelujah! Jamie said you were pretty sure you were going to accept.'

'I was.'

'What made you change your mind?'

'He did—or, rather, the things he said cleared my mind enough to make me realise I was about to make the wrong decision.' Casey's sherry-coloured eyes narrowed thoughtfully. 'When I left London in the first place, my sister Megan accused me of running away from things I couldn't handle, but she was wrong. But if I'd taken this job, I would have been guilty of exactly that. I didn't want the job and I didn't want the lifestyle that would have gone with it—but I just didn't see how I could go on living here.'

'Because of Jamie?' Lisa cut in softly.

'Jamie—and Fantasy. Losing them both all but devastated me,' she said with painful honesty. 'I haven't known agony like that since my parents died.' She gave a tiny, unconscious shrug. 'To tell you the truth, I haven't got over that, maybe I never will completely. But I realise now that I won't recover any better by going off to London—in fact I'd probably make matters worse for myself. At least here I'm in a place I love—and perhaps that will be the best cure in the long run.' She paused, staring into her coffee-cup. 'However, this house really is too full of painful memories—I don't think I can ever feel comfortable here again after all that's happened.'

'So you're looking for a place to buy?'

'Correct.'

'Any joy so far?'

Casey shook her head disgustedly. 'I spent all day yesterday driving about from one end of the county to the other, in a totally wild-goose chase. That's probably why I feel—and look—so wrecked today. None of the places I looked at bore any resemblance to the estate agent's descriptions.'

'Well, never mind.' Lisa laid down her cup decisively. 'Put it out of your mind for today.'

'Why?' Casey eyed her warily, sensing her friend was about to spring something on her.

'Because, as you've doubtless forgotten, this is the day of the local show.'

Casey gave a tiny grimace. 'You're quite right, I had forgotten. But it doesn't matter, since I'm not going.'

'Yes, you are.' Lisa's look of determination warned her not to bother arguing. 'You owe it to the village.'

'Come again?'

'Don't you realise people will come from miles around just to see if our celebrity will be there?'

Casey gave a little snort of laughter. 'Don't be ridiculous!'

'I'm serious! We're likely to get the best turn-out we've ever had this year, and that'll be great for village funds.' Lisa laid a cajoling hand on Casey's arm. 'You wouldn't really let us down, would you?'

'Well, I——'

'Good lass.' Lisa's expression changed from pleading to smug in the flash of an eye, and Casey chuckled resignedly, perfectly aware she'd been outmanoeuvred. 'Now, have some breakfast, then go and jump in the shower. I'll come back for you later.'

A thought occurred to Casey and she lifted suspicious eyes to Lisa. 'Jamie won't be there, will he?' Even after the thaw in their relations, she wasn't at all sure she could handle seeing him again.

'Jamie?' Lisa shook her blonde head. 'I think he's on duty today.'

Casey relaxed. 'OK, I will come. What should I wear?'

'Something comfortable. A pair of jeans—or, better still, wear your jodhpurs.'

'Don't people get dressed up for the show?'

Lisa scoffed. 'Don't be daft! If you see any frocks wandering about they'll be on the backs of tourists.'

They chatted for a few minutes more, then Lisa excused herself, saying she still had some farm chores to attend to before she could justifiably give herself the rest of the day off. Left alone, Casey saw to her own household tasks and had a shower, then walked slowly through to the bedroom to change.

Feeling a strange reluctance, she pulled her jodhpurs from a drawer, a lump instantly forming in her throat as she recalled the times she'd worn them. For long moments she simply clutched the garment, breathing in the faint scent of horse still clinging to the material. In her mind she saw herself, seated astride Fantasy's back, hanging on for dear life, a mere passenger as the mare hurtled round the green field. Then she saw Jamie standing in the centre of the field calling out instructions as she tried valiantly to obey. Finally she saw Jamie on the bay gelding Spud, galloping ahead of her like the wind as Fantasy flew along behind, her silvery mane and tail streaming out like banners, and the vision brought hot stinging tears to her eyes.

By the time Lisa arrived, however, she was dressed in the jodhpurs and a white cotton shirt, all signs of her sorrow hidden beneath a light covering of make-up.

'You look fine.' The other woman nodded

approvingly. 'Take your hard hat—you never know, someone might ask you to ride.'

Casey paled at the thought. 'I don't think so,' she said. 'I really don't want——'

'Good lord, girl, have you given up horses for life?'

'No, but——'

'Well, then, you have to get over Fantasy some time. This is as good a time as any.' Lisa softened her tone. 'I know it's tough and that you were very fond of the mare, but you have to take the first steps, Casey.'

Casey nodded dully. 'I suppose you're right.'

'Of course I am. Now grab your jacket and let's get going. I want to drag Joe round the stalls at least once before he disappears into the beer tent.'

The show-site was just outside the village, reached by a road Casey rarely had occasion to use. By the time they reached it the place was a hive of activity, and Casey's eyes widened as she surveyed the scene, taking in the rows of horseboxes parked in one field, the gaily striped marquees, and the sheer volume of people present.

'I thought you said it was a small show,' she turned on Lisa accusingly.

'It is. Though I must admit it has grown a lot over the years. The fine weather's obviously brought the crowds out today.'

'Let's wander over towards the horseboxes,' Casey suggested. 'I love to watch the horses being made ready.'

To her surprise Lisa shook her head. 'No, we

might get in the way. Look, there's a class already
in progress—let's go watch it instead.'

They made their way across the showground, a
fairly lengthy task since Casey was recognised by
several different people and obligingly stopped to
chat to them and sign autographs.

'Got your pony entered in anything today, lass?'
one old farmer enquired. 'We've heard you're something of a horsewoman.'

Casey shook her head. 'Enthusiastic, but not very
talented,' she returned with a self-deprecating smile.
'No, I'm afraid Fantasy isn't here today, she's——'

'Do excuse us,' Lisa cut in suddenly, grabbing
Casey by the arm. 'I've just seen someone we must
talk to. Do you mind if I drag Casey away?'

The old man shook his head goodnaturedly. 'No,
no. On you go, lasses, and enjoy yourselves.'

'What was that for?' hissed Casey as Lisa led her
away. 'You haven't seen anyone at all, have you?'

'Nope.' The pale blue eyes were alight with
suppressed mischief. 'But I do know that old fellow.
He'd still have been standing there talking to you
this time next week if I hadn't rescued you.'

They found seats on straw bales at the side of the
showing ring and sat down to enjoy the delightful
spectacle of a Shetland pony class in action. The
hairy little creatures, proud as punch despite their
diminutive size, trotted importantly round the ring,
tugging their respective owners.

'I can't helping laughing.' Casey turned to Lisa,
her eyes dancing with mirth. 'They're just so
comical.'

Lisa nodded. 'Especially when you see a tiny kid

sat on one—it's like a Thelwell cartoon come to life. But don't be misled by their cuteness—those ponies are sturdy little characters, with guts and stamina way out of proportion to their size.'

She launched into a story about a Shetland she'd once owned, but halfway through it Casey stiffened, her eyes narrowing as she gazed over to the far side of the showground.

'I could swear I've just seen Fantasy,' she said urgently.

Lisa shrugged. 'It's possible. There are two classes especially for Arabs. The owner may have entered her.' She slid Casey a sympathetic look. 'But there are many grey horses, you know.'

Casey shook her head impatiently. 'I'd know Fantasy anywhere.' She got to her feet, but Lisa tugged her back down.

'You'll soon find out if you're right or not,' she said. 'The Arab showing class is next but one in this ring.'

Casey sat through the next class in a fever of impatience, barely seeing the beautiful Fell ponies with their incredibly luxuriant manes and tails, applauding automatically as the judge called in the winners and handed out rosettes. At the entrance to the ring the entrants for the next class were already gathering, and her eyes scanned the distinctive dished Arab faces anxiously.

'She's not there.' Disappointment hollowed in her stomach as she slumped back on to the prickly straw bale.

'Is this who you're looking for, by any chance?' An amused male voice spoke quietly behind her and she whirled round, her mouth falling open in total astonishment at the sight of a broadly grinning Jamie—and at his side, whickering gently in greeting, the grey mare Fantasy.

'Jamie! What on earth——? What's going on?'

'Never mind all that now,' Jamie returned. 'Just stand up like a good girl and let me tie your number on.'

'Number?' Bemused, she tried to twist round to see the white plastic square he was knotting round her back. 'What's this for?'

'Every entrant needs one,' he said patiently, as if explaining to a child.

'But I haven't entered anything!'

'No—but I have. I put you and Fantasy in for this class. You should have a good chance of winning it too.' He gave her a friendly wink. 'Don't worry about the entry fee, you can repay me later.'

'But what about her owner? Doesn't he mind?' Casey was beginning to seriously wonder if the whole world had gone mad.

Jamie and Lisa shared a smile. 'I think we can safely say the owner's delighted,' Lisa answered for both of them.

'Now get going—it looks as if they're holding the class up for you.' Jamie put the mare's lead-rope into her nerveless fingers and gave her a gentle shove.

'But I don't even know what to do! I've never been in a showing class before.'

'Just do as the judge tells you. Fantasy knows the ropes.' Jamie's words floated after her as she led the

mare towards the ring entrance, smiling apologetically at the other entrants as she took her place
in line.

'Good lass,' she murmured as the pony's white
ears pricked up expectantly. 'You obviously know
what to do even if I don't. Just keep me right,
sweetheart.'

Keeping one anxious eye on the judge, a
commanding-looking woman in tweeds and brogue
shoes, Casey walked round the ring behind the
others. There were six in the class, to her nervous
eye all perfect animals. One, a finely boned chestnut
mare, wouldn't settle, and danced round the ring
instead of walking, snatching at the lead-rope as her
owner tried to calm her down. Fantasy sent the
other mare a disdainful look, snorting scornfully at
her antics.

'I want you to lead your ponies up for me, please,'
the lady judge called, her voice clear and
authoritative.

The butterflies in Casey's stomach increased a
thousandfold as she waited her turn, but she needn't
have worried—Fantasy trotted out at her side like a
true daughter of the desert, her tail held high, head
carriage as proud as a queen's. Casey caught sight
of Jamie and Lisa at the ringside, Lisa holding up
both thumbs in a victory gesture, and for the first
time she began to enjoy herself. Fantasy might no
longer belong to her, but she was an animal to glory
in, and as they returned to the line-up she patted
the smooth grey neck, feeling a rush of love so
strong it threatened to choke her.

Moments later, after deliberating with another

woman, the judge began calling in the winners. Fantasy was awarded second place, and Casey led her forward, as thrilled as an Olympic medal-winner.

'Well done!' Lisa flung her arms round Casey's neck when she returned to the ringside. 'You both looked terrific.'

'Thanks.' Casey's sherry-coloured eyes were sparkling, her cheeks flushed with pleasure. 'Where's her owner? I must thank him for letting me show her.'

To her surprise, Jamie and Lisa looked a trifle shamefaced. Jamie was practically shuffling his feet, like an embarrassed schoolboy.

'What's going on?' Casey demanded suspiciously. 'Where's Fantasy's owner?'

'Well, actually,' Jamie made a show of clearing his throat, 'you're looking at him.'

'What?' Casey's voice rose an octave on the single word.

'It's not so difficult to understand.' His face lit up in a grin. 'I've bought her.'

'You have? But why?'

'Why?' he echoed softly. 'For a lot of reasons. But the most important one is that I bought her for you. I want you to have your Fantasy.'

Casey felt as though the ground had tilted beneath her, as though the world had slipped off its axis.

'But that's crazy,' she said wonderingly. 'Why would you do such a thing?'

Gently he stroked a finger down her cheek, and his touch sent a tremor through her body. 'To apologise,' he said softly. 'To say I've been wrong.'

She gave a shaky little laugh. 'Mister, you sure picked an expensive way to apologise! In any case, you've already said you're sorry.'

'I didn't think mere words were enough after the way I treated you.'

Casey shook her head in a bid to sort out her addled thoughts. 'It really wasn't necessary, you know—if you'd told me the owner wanted to sell, I'd have bought her back myself.'

'I know you would.' His dark eyes held a mixture of things, almost impossible to decipher, but they were turning Casey's knees to water. 'I realised that when I saw you crying for her in the field. I'd never known until then just how much she meant to you.' He chuckled. 'And she wasn't actually for sale— let's just say I persuaded the owner she was surplus to requirements.'

'Jamie!' Her eyes widened in horror. 'What did you do to the poor man?'

He held up his hands in surrender. 'Nothing terrible, I promise you. When I left you that day, I telephoned the police and asked them for his name and address—it wasn't hard to track down a farmer who'd had a pony called Annabel stolen.' His eyes twinkled. 'Then I went to see him—and I think my offer to buy came at just the right time. His daughter's gone off to college and doesn't have time to ride any more, and I reckon he'd been feeling guilty ever since taking Fantasy away from you. "Never did see a lass looking so damn sad," he told me.' He looked deep into her eyes and she felt a warmth flooding her body from her toes upwards.

'I hate to break into this touching scene,' Lisa cut

in drily, 'but if you two are about to fall into each other's arms, might I volunteer to take the pony for a walk? I don't think either of us is ready for such an X-rated scene.'

Casey nodded vaguely, barely hearing her friend's words as she led the mare away.

'You don't have to give her to me, you know,' she murmured, as Jamie's hand came up to cup her face, his long fingers warm against her skin. 'I'll buy her from you.'

'No, you won't. I want you to feel beholden to me.'

She frowned, puzzled. 'Why?'

His lips curved into a smile and her heart contracted with longing to feel them once again against her own.

'Because I want to stack up the odds against your leaving me.'

'Leaving you?' Casey could only whisper the words, barely able to believe what she was hearing.

Jamie nodded solemnly. 'Did I forget to mention that part of the deal? I want you with me Casey—forever. I can't offer you any more than my father offered my mother, but——'

'I never wanted any more,' she whispered, her voice made husky by tears gathering in her throat.

'Then you won't leave? You won't take the job in London?'

'I've already turned it down.' She couldn't help but laugh at his look of astonishment. 'So, you see, you went to very unnecessary expense.'

He shook his head. 'Not unnecessary. Fantasy belongs with you.'

'Even though I'm a city girl?' Her eyes laughed up into his and he grasped her by the shoulders, shaking her gently.

'Not any more. In any case, I love you, city girl—I think I have ever since I saw you trying to trot the pony up for me in those ridiculous high-heeled shoes!'

'And I love you, vet-man,' she breathed, the joy of being able to say the words aloud to him making her feel quite light-headed. 'Oh, so very much!'

His head dipped towards her and, though he was blocking out the sun, Casey felt its warm rays exploding in her heart as his mouth met hers, his caress tender, yet infinitely more exciting than anything she had ever known. Ignoring the people surrounding them, he closed his arms about her, holding her with a fierce possessiveness that made wild voices sing in her blood.

'And now. . .' eternities later he lifted his head to gaze deep into her eyes '. . .I have to go and get ready for the victory parade.' Her puzzled expression made him smile. 'Wise up, city girl,' he teased gently. 'That's when all the prize-winners parade round the main ring.'

'But you haven't won anything.'

'Oh, yes, I have.' His dark eyes gleamed. 'I've won the finest prize any man could hope for—and I can promise you here and now, I won't ever let her go.'

HISTORICAL

CHRISTMAS

STORIES · 1991

Bring back heartwarming memories of Christmas past,
with Historical Christmas Stories 1991, a collection of
romantic stories by three popular authors:

Christmas Yet To Come
by Lynda Trent
A Season of Joy
by Caryn Cameron
Fortune's Gift
by DeLoras Scott
A perfect Christmas gift!

HARLEQUIN
Romance

A Christmas tradition...

Imagine spending Christmas in New Orleans with a blind stranger and his aged guide dog—when you're supposed to be there on your honeymoon!
#3163 Every Kind of Heaven
by Bethany Campbell

Imagine spending Christmas with a man you once "married"—in a mock ceremony at the age of eight!
#3166 The Forgetful Bride
by Debbie Macomber

Available in December 1991, wherever Harlequin books are sold.

RXM

HARLEQUIN
PROUDLY PRESENTS
A DAZZLING NEW CONCEPT IN ROMANCE FICTION

One small town—twelve terrific love stories

Welcome to Tyler, Wisconsin—a town full of people
you'll enjoy getting to know, memorable friends and
unforgettable lovers, and a long-buried secret that
lurks beneath its serene surface....

JOIN US FOR A YEAR IN THE LIFE OF TYLER

Each book set in Tyler is a self-contained love story;
together, the twelve novels stitch the fabric of a
community.

LOSE YOUR HEART TO TYLER!

The excitement begins in March 1992, with
WHIRLWIND, by Nancy Martin. When lively, brash
Liza Baron arrives home unexpectedly, she moves
into the old family lodge, where the silent and
mysterious Cliff Forrester has been living in seclusion
for years....

WATCH FOR ALL TWELVE BOOKS
OF THE TYLER SERIES
Available wherever Harlequin books are sold

HARLEQUIN

Romance

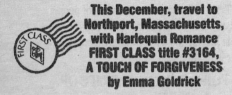

**This December, travel to
Northport, Massachusetts,
with Harlequin Romance
FIRST CLASS title #3164,
A TOUCH OF FORGIVENESS
by Emma Goldrick**

Folks in Northport called Kitty the meanest woman in town,
but she couldn't forget how they had duped her brother and
exploited her family's land. It was hard to be mean, though,
when Joel Carmody was around—his calm, good humor
made Kitty feel like a new woman. Nevertheless, a Carmody
was a Carmody, and the name meant money and power to
the townspeople.... Could Kitty really trust Joel, or was he
like all the rest?

If you missed September title #3149, ROSES HAVE THORNS (England), October title
#3155, TRAPPED (England) or November title #3159, AN ANSWER FROM THE HEART
(England) and would like to order any of them, send your name, address, zip or postal
code, along with a check or money order for $2.99 plus 75¢ postage and handling ($1.00
in Canada) for each book ordered, payable to Harlequin Reader Service to:

In the U.S.
3010 Walden Avenue
P.O. Box 1325
Buffalo, NY 14269-1325

In Canada
P.O. Box 609
Fort Erie, Ontario
L2A 5X3

Please specify book title(s) with your order.
Canadian residents add applicable federal and provincial taxes.

JT-B12R